# Warning


## GAY DRAMA WITH HEA

Gay Fiction / Mature-Bear Romance / Sports Theme / Starting All Over / Mental Challenged / Healing / Adult Content / Slow Burn / Heat Leve 3.5

This book contains varying degrees of explicit homosexual scenes and adult language. It is intended for sale to adults ONLY, as defined by the laws of the country in which you made your purchase. Please store your files wisely, where they cannot be accessed by under-aged readers.


## POSSIBLE TRIGGERS

## Language / Drama / Explicit Sexual Content / Loss & Coping

# DEDICATION

To my other half, that I will always feel you, both with me and your absence. And to our Bug and Bobcat

A HUGE HUGE THANK YOU and Super Squishy Bear Hug to all our readers out there!!! Without you, we'd just be a lonely book on the shelf.

Special Thanks goes to:

Alison Greene & Ethan Ljubankovic

for keeping me Dyslexic-Disaster-Zone free.

And to my Beta Readers:

Jay Cam, Tom Tanyon, and Ethan LJubankovic

# TRADEMARK ACKNOWLEDGEMENT

Following Trademark &/or copyrighted name brand products have been either mentioned or used fictitiously in this story.

<u>Films:</u>

The Incredibles - Pixar Animation Studios and Walt Disney Pictures

Star Wars – Lucas Films and Walt Disney Pictures

Empire Strikes Back – A Star Wars Film – Lucas Films and Walt Disney Pictures

Star Trek – Paramount Pictures

Willy Wonka – Paramount Pictures

<u>Misc. Products:</u>

Body Tech Light-Weight Workout Pants by Monsta Performance Clothing Co.

Harley Davidson BossHoss Motorcycles

Otomix Fitness shoes

Colt 10-Function Vibe Buzz Rider by Colt Gear

Timberland Boots

Oreo Cookies by Nabisco

<u>Athletic Competitions:</u>

Strongman Challenge

Iron Man

Olympics

Highlander Games

Timber Challenge

# Big Spoon & Teddy Bear

TARIAN P.S.

# Big Spoon & Teddy Bear

## THE TEDDY BEAR COLLECTION
## TARIAN P.S.

Gay Fiction / Mature-Bear Romance / Sports Theme / Healing / Adult Content

For years Gage has been turning men into steel, athletes into warriors of strength, competitors into medalists. But Gage isn't looking for any more empty trophies, he's looking for something far more meaningful.

When Gage takes a new job at an old gym, he doesn't expect his entire life to get a workout, just a change of pace. At first it doesn't seem like much and about the only plus is the endless view of rugged and well worked man-candy in the form of weightlifters and Strongman competitors that he'd be training and working with. He figures he has it made the minute he walks in the front door in that sense. But in truth, it isn't enough. He wants a place to set down roots. More importantly, he wants some*one* to take root with.

Because he's gay, Gage had always been told to just be happy with what he got, but there's something about the gym manager, Boomer. A quiet, towering mountain of a Bear that Gage hoping for more than just daydreaming about the large furry physique. And that alone promises to put a spark back into the life of a lonely, freckled ginger.

You're never too old for a teddy bear, right?

# TABLE OF CONTENT

Gage pulled up along the curb, behind the souped-up silver Honda with a glossy top wax finish and parked his bike. He leaned the Harley BossHoss onto its kickstand, stretched, and then drew his leg over the seat, giving the massive building he'd just pulled up in front of, a once over. The sign above the door said GYM and that was it. No fancy add-ons, no franchise logos, just GYM. His gaze drifted over the cracks in the brick mortar to the peeling paint. Where his thoughts had gone, he wasn't really sure. Until now, they were berating him for sending his resume here. Didn't make any sense to give up a career clientele of future *Mr. Universes* and skin-models for start-over at a rundown, hole-in-the-wall place out on the shirttails of the Jersey hood. However, now that he was here, all those second-guessings just up and vanished. Sure, he would still be training, but the diva side of the industry didn't exist here.

The front door swung open, and several men came out, gym bags in hands and skin glistening with sweat earned from a hard work out. Not even the pretty boys of Hollywood-ville, which would have showered to rid themselves of that rewarding sheen, looked so welcoming for Gage's preference of eye candy as what just walked out the door here. Instead, Gage was the ringside viewer of big thick bodies, plus a few burly types, unafraid to smell like men. The display brought a lusty grin to mind. *Here*, on the farthest side of the continental US from Hollywood, the view was considerably better, at least the gym membership was. The building not so much. Still, it was something he was in dire need of. *Besides*, he nodded some form of approval to himself, glancing down the sidewalk to the rows of Brownstones down at the bottom of the hill, and the group of boys playing stick ball in the street— *this felt real.*

"Haha— check out fool boy." A tall, built black man came up the sidewalk with a crew of pals, gloating over his remark with a smug grin, and pointed in Gage's direction.

Gage felt the chuff-like chuckle in his chest, watching as the man and his pals went inside. *Fool? Ha! Challenge accepted*, he thought to himself, and headed in to meet his new boss.

Inside was the heavenly smell of men, men, and more men— and every damn one of them heavily perfumed with sweat, musk, and testosterone. There was a group of five helping one another change the plates on one of the two inclined leg presses, just to his right. Further down the wall, one man around college age was looking at his reflection in the mirror, training his thoughts to see the lift. His fingers lacing and flexing around the bar with what looked to be about 250lbs of dead weight black iron on each end. While two others, who looked to be a few years older, stood nearby at the ready for spotting duty.

Scattered throughout the assembly of machines and racks of weights were others. Across the gym, heading towards, what appeared to be a boxing ring, was the guy who'd called Gage *fool boy*. But rather than taking up with a group of guys hanging around the ring, the new arrivals took over a row of overhead bars. They wasted no time, bags tossed aside and three of the men jumped up catching a bar, and like they were in a race, began rapid pull-ups, army style.

Unlike all the weights in the racks that all weighed in on the heavy side, the men came in every shape, size, and color. The gym's interior was a bit dark and a whole lot worn down, but not at all lacking in equipment. Dead weights sat on various racks along one mirrored wall, ring cables hung from the ceiling in a corner, medicine balls, benches, and mats for floor workouts in another corner. A fairly new and good sized twenty station octagon cross core system was resurrected halfway toward the back with various hanging straps, bars, and pulleys.

Someone shouting pulled his attention further to the back where the boxing ring took up much of the rear space of an adjacent room, no doubt filled with a variety of punching bags and accessories just out of his line of sight. The two sections of the gym were partitioned off by a crumbling wall of painted cinderblock with an elephant sized doorway that connected them.

Gage's overall scan of the place revealed that while there were plenty of machines to suit various forms of training, there was no sign of a perky Biff and Barbie hanging about to sell you on the latest greatest fitness machines with an exuberant membership plan and guilt you into losing another ten pounds or you weren't perfect. From what Gage could make out, there was plenty of extra meat per pound to be had here.

Then there were the things that one didn't see in the average gym. For starters, from front to rear along the far wall was a weight-sled track with a harness on one end and a flat vertical plate on the other.

Where the track ended, just before the boxing area, was a small springboard stage along with some of the heaviest racks of weights a person would ever see a man lift.

And anywhere along the walls, where there weren't mirrors— were action posters of large, beefy men— running with kegs in hand— pulling tractors— flipping phone poles while wearing kilts. The words Ironman— Strongman— and Timber Tossing Competition screamed out at him in bold fonts. All but the one poster tacked to the wall next to the door where Gage stood. He stared at the cartoon scene of a well pumped-up character with two train boxcars on ripcord, arm pulleys as weights. Instead of Ironman or the like, the caption read: *The Incredibles*. Gage grinned, he didn't recognize the suggested cartoon, but obviously the place had a sense of humor, too.

"Can I help you?"

Gage glanced over his shoulder, finding he'd been addressed by the man behind the counter. He was standing there, leaning towards the glass-cased counter with both hands on the edge taking his relaxed weight. Gage's gaze immediately went to the man's hair, which had long since gone gray, buzzed damn near to the scalp. A little more and the man'd be the epitome of *Mr. Clean*, except maybe for the septum nose piercing this guy had. Thick muscular arms matched his equally thick midsection. *Someone clearly liked his pot roast as much as he liked the gym.* A silver mat of chest hair curled out from behind his tank top, which had been cut down to reveal a little more; including a glint of metal that Gage guessed could only be a pierced nipple ring peeking out the side of the muscle tank. The shirt boasted a *Gold's Gym* logo with a large, self-expressed X over it in black magic-marker.

Gage turned on the professional attitude and stepped over. "Yeah, I'm looking for Schiller."

"You got 'em. You my new guy?" He said it like Gage was always meant to be there.

"Yep." Gage nodded, feeling a bit of a comforting smile creep over his face. The place was already warming up to him and he was liking the feel of it more and more, though he could not explain why had he tried. But it *was* happening.

Schiller closed up the register, locked it, and then waved Gage to follow him, "Come on back."

Gage came around the counter and followed Schiller down the hall, noting the rest of man's attire as he did. Schiller had on a pair of gray loose fit performance pants, his Otomix shoes standing out with their new whiteness. *At least Schiller wasn't wearing the fad kickboxing linen pants, Gage was so sick to death of seeing back west.* To Gage, those things were always a red flag for posers. But he didn't get the feeling any one here was of the same cut.

They passed a couple of doors on his left, and then went into the office at the very end. First glance and Gage realized the boss man didn't need a trainer; he needed a secretary or just someone with enough gonads to come in here and just start tossing shit.

On every item, that once upon a time had a surface, were papers— magazines— file folders— newspapers— an occasional brown paper bag from perhaps a lunch stuffed in between, and who knew what else— stacked as high as gravity allowed. And more stacked up every few feet all along the floor, against the wall, on top of filing cabinets. Over on another table or corner desk were more leaning towers of paper sundries.

Schiller grabbed a stack of newspapers to clear the chair in front of his desk for Gage. He motioned to it with his burdened arm before finding a spot on the floor to drop his load and then sat down behind the desk. He looked Gage over and then started his employer spiel right off the bat.

"Now, here's the lay of the land. I come in and open the place up. Around lunch time, Boomer, who's the manager, comes in and works until closing. Once he's here, I leave whenever I damn well feel like it. Your job is in training, not managing. Most of your clients are gonna be weightlifters and Strongman competitors. Quite a few of them are in the nationals, so don't be taking them lightly. You also got a few kids and you're not to be pissin' them down either." He paused to scratch as his chest a moment, then with a fresh supply of air resumed the long-winded speech. "Now Harrison owns the boxing ring, so you don't have to mess with it, but he's got a few boxers and wrestlers trying to go pro, and he might ask to have you running them through the gauntlet at times. Don't worry, if he asks, he's already paid, Boomer has seen to it he never tries to scam my trainers ever again." Schiller stopped a moment seemingly to look Gage up and down a moment, his body hiccupped with a slight chuckle, "Anybody ever tell you, you're covered, and I mean covered, in freckles?"

Gage smirked, "I'm certain once or twice someone has." And it was the truth. Aside from his bright pumpkin-orange hair, he was, in fact, covered, and rather heavily, head to toe, and then some, with a mix of light and dark-orange heavy splotches of freckles. His mom used to call him *Pumpkin Spice* when he was little just so he wouldn't feel so out of place; a boyish nickname that only he used for his own amusement now.

Schiller nodded, a brief pause to retrace where he was in his routine, and then carried on. "Now, most of the boys come in later in the day, after school or work. So that's when you need to be here. And it's your job to clean up the equipment at the end of the night. So, you and Harrison will be the last ones out every night." Schiller dropped an elbow pointedly on the desk and looked Gage dead in the eye with a cocked brow. "We close at seven. Not nine, not ten, not twenty-four-hours— *seven*. This isn't a fitness gym for people to come and work-out when it's convenient for them. If they are serious about their training, they see to it our hours fit into their schedule. Now, if you'll be needing a night off, do not go looking to Boomer to cover your closing. Boomer leaves at seven on the dot, Monday through Friday. If you let me know at least a few days in advance, I can get you covered. Are we clear on that part?"

Gage nodded, not entirely sure of the relevance, but okay, *Boomer doesn't cover. Got it.*

Schiller nodded, satisfied this wasn't an issue and sat back, and went on. "It's up to you to keep track of your schedule. Won't no one be holding your hand and passing out any print outs. Scheduler is behind the counter, sitting on the table thingy, and when someone calls in or makes an appointment as they leave, it goes in the book. So best get in the habit to look at it every night before you go. Now, if you want to make some extra money you can book more clients in the mornings, just so long as you know you're still closing."

Again, Gage nodded.

"Another thing, if you want to work out either before you start for the day or after we close up that's fine.

Just clean up and lock up before you go." Schiller pitched forward in his chair and pulled a drawer open, he reached in, and then tossed a set of keys to Gage. "Those are the keys for the front door, gate, and stock room. I'll have Boomer get you a locker."

Gage held the keys up in his hand, looking them over. Just like that, he was given access to the place. He glanced over at Schiller unsure how he'd managed to earn the guy's trust so quickly.

"Oh, and one last thing. Stay the hell away from Boomer. Don't get in his way, don't mess with him, and don't go thinking it's your goal to best him at anything. If you do, I ain't gonna bother firing you just to save your ass from getting a beating."

Gage hadn't really meant to ask the blatant question, but once it came out, there was no going back, "Pardon my judgment, boss, but uh, if he's that bad, why have him as manager?"

Schiller pushed back, tipping his desk chair as far as it would go. His arm swung out toward the window behind him, his hand snatched the cord to the blinds with accuracy and yanked on it. A quick zip exposed the window, putting the gym on the other side on display. "See that shit out there? That's every street thug who wants to pack his own guns. Every Latino that thinks he's the next Roberto Duran or Julio Chavez, and every parolee trying to play it straight and they come here to let off steam." Schiller let the cord go and the blinds fell back into place, shutting out the view. The owner glanced at Gage with one of those looks like he had the inside scoop on everything, "Somewhere in all that is a kid trying to make it to the Olympics. *Boomer* keeps the peace."

Gage chuckled, "Maybe he needs a better girlfriend."

Schiller eased back in his chair, rocking, "Wouldn't do him much good. Boomer doesn't fly straight." He smirked, shaking his head mildly.

Gage's gaydar attentiveness immediately perked up, "Boomer is gay and no one harasses him for it?"

It was the owner's turn to laugh now, grabbing his pencil out of habit and scribbled on a pad on his desk, before glancing up at Gage. "Nobody makes fun of Boomer. That is, if the sorry sap wants to keep his car and his body intact."

It seemed like all the bases had been covered in a manner of efficiency and the interview would be drawing to a close here soon and it was just that suddenly Gage wasn't sure he'd landed the right gym for himself. *Street thugs and parolees. Really?*

Gage just kind of slunk down in his seat then, not sure of what he was wanting. He'd left a high paying job working with *Mr. Universe* wannabes and mindless beefcakes. He came looking for something new— but winding up in some run-down gym for street thug rejects working under a dodgy manager wasn't what he had in mind either. Not even the promising eye candy could make up for this. He wiped across his face just under his nose with the broad web of his thumb and forefinger— thinking it out, but Schiller beat him to the punch.

"Why are you here, son?" He sat back waiting for Gage's answer.

Gage still wasn't entirely sure of his answer. He had grown so numb from all the flash and glam in California. The whole world seemed plastic and generic. Nothing was real or important, nothing fulfilling. Always about more muscle, more glitter, more tanning bronzer, more trophies— but none of them meant *anything*. Having looked out the window while Schiller named off the slummers' flipside version of the same thing, Gage wasn't sure he was going to find whatever the hell it was he *was* looking for here either. About the only good it offered was a job with better Beefy eye-candy.

"Yeah, alright. Why don't you just toss me them keys back?" Schiller sat back up, his chair creaking underneath him as he did, and held his hand out. The disappointment marring the man's aged face.

Gage was reluctant— he still needed a job too.

"This ain't no way station while you look for one of those fancy yogurt gyms. I got boys in here that needs someone to stick it out with them. And I can see right now, you ain't the one."

Gage was certain there might have been more to the lecture, but it was interrupted when someone knocked on the door. The very delivery of *said knock* was like a mayday of urgency from the other side.

"Yeah!? What the hell do ya' want?" Schiller tossed his pencil down and then planted his elbow on his desk, leaning into it, waiting to hear what was on fire.

The door snapped open and a young man's head popped in. "Boomer's in and uhm— well— someone is in his parking space."

Schiller's eyes started to roll across his face like he'd had it with all the nonsense for the day, but then abruptly redirected his focus, leveling it on Gage. "Hope you have good car insurance, son."

That statement was followed by a loud creaking sound of flexing metal coming from outside— then a crash that echoed with breaking glass. The next sound to come from out front was hard to explain, but it sounded like someone was dragging metal across the asphalt.

Gage jumped out of his seat and tore out of the office like his gym-pants were on fire. He crashed into a few bodies along the way until he came stumbling out the front door just as the biggest man he'd ever laid eyes on walked past him with a rather nonchalant gait and went in where Gage had just exited. Gage managed to tear his focus from the towering, pissed-off giant and back to what he feared. But his pride and joy metallic orange Hog was still sitting pretty as could be, right where he left it. The souped-up Honda, he'd parked behind, was another story. No longer where it had been when Gage pulled up. Now it was laying on its side and, if the tell-tale trail of silver paint on the street was any indication, it had been skidded up and out of the marked parking slot. One full car space down.

"Whad'aye tell ya? Fool boy dunne known not to park in the Boomer man's handicap spot."

Gage twisted around seeing the same tall, lean, black guy he'd seen going in when he had arrived. Gage let out another one of those soft huff-like chuckles, so *Fool boy* hadn't been him after all. But rather the unlucky Honda owner.

Like the rest of the sidewalk watchers, Gage herded back in, but he paused just inside letting his eyes readjust and he dialed his attention on the giant now standing behind the counter flipping through the logbook, making a few marks in it, then headed down the hall and disappeared through one of the doors.

Once more, which was like go for three since Gage'd arrived, he was seeing something he couldn't explain, but something about the big silent man had Gage locked solid in a decision to stay. He quickly gathered his thoughts and returned to the boss man's office.

"I'll take it."

Schiller was laid back on his chair, with one of those brand-new tennis shoes propped up on one of the teetering piles of folders, and one solo folder in his hand. "I don't have any positions open for temps. I need someone who can duke it out with these kids. Most of 'em don't have a hope in hell, save for this gym. Don't nobody give a shit about any of these social reject kids. Hell, some of 'em ain't even got caring parents. This gym is their ticket out of here. So, I need someone to invest in those tickets." Schiller didn't even bother to look up when he tossed the folder from his hand to his desk and fetched another from a random stack.

"And you'll never find anyone better trained to get them to their goals." Gage sucked in a deep breath with a sound that flared from his nostrils like a bull readying to argue the point.

Schiller twisted around in his chair and dropped the folder from his hand to the desk with a slap. "Give me one good reason why I ought to pick you over all these others?" He waved his hands over the files.

Gage smirked, using the only thing he had. "Because I already have the keys."

Schiller narrowed his gaze on him, studying him, but in what form Gage was uncertain. Then, out of nowhere, without any prior indication, the man burst out with a clucky kind of laugh. Like some inside joke he failed to share. "Alright kid, see you Monday. Now get the fuck out of my office. I have to call all these sorry saps and tell 'em the job's been filled."

# 2

With his new job in hand, Gage headed home without an introduction to the manager, Boomer. Schiller said he'd rather have Boomer in a good mood; it was just better for everyone involved. Gage didn't rightly care, but he soaked up another good look of the solid beef on his way out. Call him shallow, but Boomer had been Gage's reason for taking the job. Seven years in LA dealing with the stardom side of body building had done nothing for Gage's dick. He made money, but that was about it. And just like anyone else out there, he squandered most of it. Now, he had little to show for it.

He dropped a hand from the handlebars to pat the side of the tank as he cruised down the road. He at least had his dream bike, and had enough money stashed away that he'd been able to buy a small rinky-dink house to keep a roof over his head with just enough left over to help get by if times got lean. But there were no trophies on his wall to boast about, no champions from out west that he'd cared to claim to have had a hand in the making. And most of all, no man to say was his. Which right about now, he would settle for just someone to burn the sheets with.

He stopped at the local grocer, picking up some grub and a few pints for the night. Even here, it was a world away from where he left. A little more run down than what he had planned, but like the gym, it was well lived in. Here people stressed over making the rent, keeping the kid in school, health care, and maybe saving up enough for a weekend getaway to the shores. It was funny because, as worn down and aged the area seemed, it was a bit of fresh air from where he'd just come from; where the value of life was summed up in the latest silicone job and who was seen with whom in the daily gossip column.

Gage filled the plastic grocery basket with some hamburger buns, meat, and the trimmings—grabbed two pints of cheap beer, snatched a bag of chips, and brought it all up to the register. There was a basket of apples right there and he grabbed one and added it just before the woman at the register tallied him up.

"That'll be twenty, sixty-three."

Gage already had his wallet out and he pulled out enough bills to cover it and handed them over.

The woman took them, giving him a peculiar glance. "Say, ain't you the big fella that moved into ol' Dean's house on the end of Farbour Street?"

Gage took his change and dropped in his pocket, "Yeah, that's me."

"I'm Darlayne, two houses up across the way."

Gage shook his head, not getting a picture in his head.

"My husband, Tyrese, rides," she added.

That's when it hit him. "The raked-out rat bike."

She nearly choked out a laugh at his comment then tried to hide it, "You dunno the half of it." She rolled her eyes and waved her hand downwards.

"I'm surprised you noticed or remember me."

"You're kinda hard to miss. Aside that your hair is like the brightest orange I've ever seen in natural color, but you are also nearly the size of a brownstone. Tyrese took one look at you and went inside to drag out the bar bells from the garage." She cocked an eyebrow up at him in an approving expression, "You're a good man to have around, so welcome to the neighborhood."

Gage grinned. It came as a surprise because the last thing he expected was for anyone to welcome him. *It was Jersey after all.* "Thanks." He grabbed his groceries and went out, loading up on his bike and headed to his new home.

*Home.*

He'd called this area home once before. Just north of here. Seven years ago, seemed like such a long time now for some reasons. So much had changed, yet still remained the same. Still familiar. So, it was easy to call it such again.

*Home.*

The house he bought wasn't much, but then he'd never needed much. A room just for him and his bed, a second room to just put *stuff* in. The open-air kitchen was separated from the living room by the eat-on countertop and just enough corner space for a small kitchen table. The living room was already consumed with the big screen tv and the large sectional sofa with twin recliners. Most importantly, the house came with a garage to lock his bike up at night.

That's all a man really needed anyways, right? A roof over his head, a bed, and a sofa to park his ass on. So why was it when he got there, he was on the sofa with his beer and chips staring at the flat screen tv, not caring that it wasn't even on. Or the hamburger meat he'd just bought went straight into the fridge, or that all his *stuff* was still in boxes?

Because he wanted more than just to be existing. Of all the men he'd turned into steel, of all the athletes he'd driven to be warriors of strength, not one of them had gone on to be something Gage held value to. Posing in front of judges to show hours spent in a gym was not a life changing event. While their physique was not an accomplishment gained without hard work, it had no purpose except to win one more trophy. Gage had no need of trophies; he was looking for purpose. And his house? It was just a place. Empty and void of meaning without somconc to share it with to make it a home. *Was it all a man needed?* Gage supposed so, but he still wanted more, and he didn't know how to find it.

# 3

Gage was at the gym, sitting back behind the counter, wolfing down his Wednesday afternoon lunch while completely fixated on Boomer's ass. A fast-becoming favorite pastime to which the big lug seemed to never take notice, which was fine by Gage, because it meant he didn't have to stop looking anytime soon.

The ringing chime on the front door was probably his next appointment. He shoveled in the last bite of his sandwich and started to push up until he saw the person who'd come in was a heavy weight girl, and he sat back down, returning his attention to Boomer's backside while he chewed.

"You're looking a tad on the slim shady side." Was Boomer's hello to her, which only got a shake of her head, signaling a form of denial for a response. Boomer apparently wasn't buying it and pointed her ass over to the scales and followed her over. There was an amusing back and forth between the two as to where the center weight on the scale bar was supposed to be, before Boomer bonked her on the head playfully and won out. But whatever that scale said had him scowling down at her.

Gage just sat back and watched it with detached amusement. He'd seen too many people her size and trying to get them down to a size that the rest of the world thought they should be was a losing battle. Nor was diet always to blame. Though he had to admit the girl's form wasn't that of a typical overweight teenager.

"You're still losing weight." Boom scolded the girl. "You can't be doing that if you are going to remain a super heavyweight contender."

"Tuh," she tossed at him.

Gage did a double take on the ensuing argument.

"Don't be *tuhuh-ing* me. You can't keep losing weight in the middle of the season. You're out of your category now. What the hell are you gonna do three weeks from now when you go in for the qualifications for regionals and you fail your category? You're out. You want that to happen?" Boomer was lecturing her.

The girl slunked her shoulders and Gage started taking a closer look at her body form now. A lot of that beef was up around her chest and shoulders. Her torso was squared down, but there wasn't much he could say about the leg mass hidden away in the swimming legs of her lightweight *Monsta brand* workout pants. But her arms looked strange— not flimsy.

"Boomer, it's been hard not having a coach," she retaliated.

"Yeah, well, we got that all worked out. Didn't you get the email?"

"Yeah— some new guy." She had all the lacking enthusiasm of any teen. Then Boomer pointed Gage's way. And his eyes locked on him. For a split second the world, the girl, and the gym blacked out. *Boomer looked at him.* Usually, Boomer acted like Gage was never there. Gage grinned at himself, dropping his gaze to the floor, and scratched at his brow a second. It was kinda fun having a puppy crush on the big bear. *Oddly new— but fun.*

"This here is, Gage." Boomer was walking up, leading the heavy-set girl with him. "Gage, this is one of your sponsored students, Skye Jackson."

Gage swiped his hands clean then reached his hand out over the front counter.

Skye accepted, shaking his hand with an unexpected strong grip. She then leaned in toward Boomer to whisper up at him for what good it did since Gage could still hear her. "He's a lot shorter than the last guy."

"Size is only a perception and like opinions they're usually way off from the truth." Boomer glanced in Gage's direction, "Skye here is one of your weightlifters." Boomer brought him up to speed, while chucking Skye in the shoulder, and then turned and walked off.

Skye stood there with a silent awkward expression. She sighed  waiting.

Gage had never trained with a girl before, so he hadn't really expected it. "How long you been training so far?"

"Three years."

"What are your goals?"

"Olympics team."

Gage's eyes went wide, "You're my super–heavyweight, Olympic-goal student?"

She nodded, wiping her hands on her pants nervously.

"Well, alright then, let's run you through a few form basics so I can see where you are, and we'll go from there."

"But I've already been taught form."

"Oh yeah? Good, so this will be a piece of cake to learn it again." He clapped his hands together then swept his arms out, waving her towards one of the racks along the mirrored wall. "Let's go."

Skye pulled up her lip on one side looking him over. "You're not tall at all. My last coach was a lot taller than you." She rolled up on the balls of her feet and stretched her chin up a touch to see if she could actually top him.

Gage allowed the chaffing. They all did it. They sized him up, finding him that at five foot and barely ten inches, he came up short. Gage widened his stance, clasped his hands in front of him, putting on his best *could-care-less* expression. The idle posture brought his massive shoulders and arms into ideal viewing without having ever flinched a single muscle to wake up and show off, "Are you here to train? If so, go check your ego at the counter. I'll be over at the platform when you're ready." He walked off. He'd batted against some of the biggest egos to prance in a gym, and he knew from experience— *never coddle them.*

Skye just stood there, gawping at him then throwing a look in Boomer's direction, who ignored the silent tantrum. There was a deep huff from Skye, a drop of her shoulders, then the inevitable surrender. She padded over where her training began, exactly as Gage had said it would.

Gage stood close, watching her form as she held her dumb bells down at her sides doing lunges, then squats, and overhead swings. Occasionally, he would tap an arm or shoulder to remind her to adjust her posture, before finally moving on to practice a few *snatches*, a matter of moving the weight bar from ground to lockout overhead. Then she was onto her *clean & jerk* lifts, a ground to chest, then to *lockout* overhead. Each movement done in less than a second.

The whole time, Skye rattled on about how the last coach didn't make her do that. And for every time she tutted him, he made her repeat the lift— *ten more times*— until her two hours were up and her ego was as sorely pissed at him as were all the muscles on her body that she hadn't been using. She was glad to be rid of him just as his next trainee arrived, or rather two trainees; a pair of twins wider than cars across the shoulders and arms as thick as some of the legs in the gym, save Gage's.

Mitch and Mike were both *Strongman Challenge* and *Iron Man* competitors, and they weren't too sweet on Gage when he put them through the same beginner steps as he'd done to Skye.

Here he was, only at the end of his third day and Gage had managed to bruise nearly a dozen egos, but he'd managed to make a point scale for his own use of where each one had been taught or maintained proper form and who hadn't. It also gave him a big fat hello to where each athlete's mind was.

Gage was used to big heads, back in LA they came in as swollen as pregnant bellies with prefabricated ideas of fame and fortune. It came with the territory being home to Hollywood and every wanna-be millionaire and movie star.

Goals weren't a bad thing, not even ones to be famous. Only sad part about it was not even half of the men he'd been put in charge of training out there wanted to commit and endure the hard work necessary to reach those goals. Oh sure, some worked hard, came in every day, but there were also the ones that came in wanting their trophies before ever having lifted the first weight from the rack. It was because of the ones in between Gage had developed a core approach to get them rolling towards their goals in a grueling training or hated him so much they rolled right back out the door to go find a more coddling coach. While Gage knew good and well he wasn't out west any more, the people here on the east coast were still people. And he expected to encounter a few of those trophy toters even here, just perhaps not as many. So, poking the bears to get at those chips on their shoulders was part of his core approach and he wasn't about to back down. He didn't care if they got mad, as long as they stuck it out. Train hard— work hard— do— repeat. But don't quit.

By Friday, Gage had met most of his regularly scheduled training clients, save for one no-show, another was out for a competition, and the two he was expecting later in the day.

Schiller reminded Gage of some movie drill sergeant. He liked to bark a lot and just like in those movies; most others didn't pay him no never mind. On his lighter side, Schiller was a storyteller and they usually had humorous plots. His jokes weren't always funny except to himself. But it broke the day up of its otherwise dull routine even if it was just to watch him get into stitches over his own jokes. Something about the laugh on that man was enough to clear a room of grey moods. Though there seldom seemed to be any. The gym had good mojo as far as Gage could tell. Everyone was doing what they were supposed to be doing, training hard, locked in on their jobs, and not screwing around. No one was in here just for the sake of having a better beach body.

The guys for the most part got along, and they often cheered each other when one was going after a really big lift. No one here was getting bottle fed, yet there was no question either that Gage was the coach in charge. Not even Boomer could be tricked into undermining him when it came to the workouts and drills Gage prescribed the trainees. A few had tested that line of scrimmage. Boomer always made it clear he managed the business; Gage managed the bodies that came inside. And it was because of this and the solid mojo of the gym that allowed Gage to oversee several guys in for training at once. Giving a little more one-on-one to each at a scheduled day and time, once or twice a week depending on their needs to observe and adjust for further development.

And right on schedule, like Schiller had said, Boomer always came in at noon.

So far, no one else had dared to park in the handicap spot, even though Gage hadn't seen anyone who did need it, use it. Nevertheless, no one had since tried to test the rules with Boomer after what'd happened to the silver Honda. Gage had, however, managed to lay claim to the spot right behind it on most days. When he couldn't, he parked on the sidewalk, refusing to let his bike be anywhere out of sight range from the front door.

Schiller sometimes hung around after Boomer got in. The two talked about this, that, and the other. People or places Gage hadn't gotten familiar with. The two covered the local current events and of course always any new stats or leads in any of the numerous strength competitions. But only rarely did they talk about the gym.

Today, Schiller took off right after Boomer got in, something about taking Charlie and Roberta out. It wasn't the first time Gage had heard the names but had yet to learn who the two were in way of Schiller's life, whether they were his kids, grandkids or a partner and kid. Gage just hadn't caught the defining words yet and Schiller didn't seem forthright about it either. So, asking hadn't crossed Gage's lips yet.

Come five o'clock, something did happen that was completely new to Gage. A white passenger van pulled up and what do you know— it parked in the handicap spot. Only this time, Boomer didn't go after it. A few minutes later and the vanload piled inside, bringing with them a roar of happy-go-lucky excitement that spread throughout the gym.

"Wow, did you see the motorcycle out front?" One of the guys in the group rushed up to Boomer who was standing behind the counter resting on his elbows while he was flipping through a magazine.

Boomer nodded.

"It's fat!" the man exclaimed excitedly, holding his arms out wide to exaggerate the width of Gage's BossHoss.

"I like orange," another of the guest group called out as if there was some form of child's play between them, and then she headed towards the back.

While the first of the group continued to carry on about the bike, the other six filed past and headed toward the back like the other and vanished inside the utility room. Then soon they all came back out with rags and bottles of chrome polish and went to work. But there was something different about their height and the way they all walked. Even their faces seemed different, but he couldn't make it out just what from across the gym.

"WHERE'S MY SUPER SUIT?!" Two guys up front near the bench presses called out in unison and soon one of the women in the group turned and responded with a wide grin.

"Why— do you need— to know?!" The women called back, jutting a round chin up in the air in a defiant posture that did nothing to hide her grin.

"Woman! You get over here and give me a hug then tell me where my suit is!" one of guys shouted back and quickly was in the arms of a fun bear hug from the woman.

Gage laughed not knowing what the super suit joke was about, but it was funny watching them, nonetheless.

"Hi! My name's Joshua."

Gage snapped around to find himself being greeted by one of the newcomers. And then he saw what was different about them. The sunken and slightly Asian eye shape was a dead giveaway. And as he glanced around, Gage could see now, they all had physical traits that came with Down syndrome. He turned back to the man who'd introduced himself as Joshua. He wasn't really young. A few crow's feet gathered around his eyes and the shadow of a long struggle in society. A deeper awareness peeped out from behind his dark eyes.

"Nice to meet you, Joshua. I'm Gage."

Joshua grinned then stepped right in past the offered handshake and gave Gage a hug.

It was awkward at first. Gage wasn't accustomed to getting hugged from strangers, but he sent the message to his brain, *this wasn't hurting him*, and he gave in with a sudden laugh and hugged Joshua back.

"You have a lot of freckles. I have a freckle. Want to see?"

Before Gage had the chance to agree Joshua was lifting his shirt sleeve to show off a quarter size birthmark on his arm.

"Wow, that's the best-looking freckle I've seen in a long time."

Joshua's grin brightened. "I have to get back to work now. It was nice meeting you."

"Nice to meet you too, Joshua."

As his new friend wandered off then stopped to start polishing the stainless steel on one of the equipment racks, Gage turned to the client he was working with, "What gives?"

Bailey smiled like he was proud of something and jutted his chin out towards the gaggle of special staff. "They come in once a week and work one hour. They do it for a couple of businesses all in this area and we sponsor an activity for them.

"What do you mean?"

You know— a movie, sometimes it's bowling, or the zoo or to a good restaurant for a birthday party. Stuff like that. We're the last of three stops for today and there are two or three other businesses they go to earlier in the week. Everyone involved chips in to sponsor a weekly activity for all of them. It's pretty cool, yanno?"

"Yeah." Gage turned and watched as they buzzed around like busy little bees. Boomer was trying to get the one that'd been all excited about the motorcycle to do some actual work, pointing, and waving him off until he finally did.

Gage had never seen anything like it before and as he watched, he realized Bailey was right, it was pretty cool. And it added to the gym's mojo.

The special team left around five after six. The extra five minutes was because Jack ran back in to tell

Boomer the big orange motorcycle was still out there and insisted Boomer come out and see it with him.

Seven o'clock arrived and Boomer locked up the offices, called out a goodnight and left the rest to Gage.

Despite the cleanup crew, Gage still went through his own routine of sanitizing the benches and hand grips on everything, then turned the lights out and left himself, rolling the steal gate into place and locking it on his way out.

He felt a little restless. Perhaps just a matter of his first week finally being established, it was a steppingstone for him. The first of many steps to building a new life here and he kind of had that need to celebrate the jitter in him. So, he hopped on his BossHoss, cranked her up, and went cruising.

He headed north towards the old haunts.

Some things had definitely changed. A few new apartment buildings had replaced some of the old warehouses that had once been taken over by the artsy people and converted into studios. He could recall a few street fairs they'd held before, often to the dislike of road traffic, but always fun to stop by and check out the creations.

Further down, something old gave way to a new movie theatre— somewhere else a new strip mall. Yet wherever he looked someone was huddled in an alcove to an old storefront's doorway, bundled up in a tattered blanket and cardboard. Maybe a pack or two of personal things tucked close to their side— A stray cat snuck from one shadow to the next— a girl strutted a little more than she needed to pine for the attention of certain drive-bys— a cop sat in his squad car seemingly oblivious to the outside world, while the siren of another could be heard in the distance. The music flavor from one red light to the next brambled back and forth from hip-hop to the latest rock. *Some things didn't change.*

He found himself just riding down one street after another, letting the nostalgia of old familiarity welcome him. He'd just taken a left and was suddenly idling his speed down until he came up on the night club he recalled from his past.

He stopped his bike just shy of the club, pausing in the street, and stared at it. A few Bears were just showing up and hanging around the door. A door man clad in fitted leather pants and a leather vest patted them down with a gloved hand, taking a freedom frisk as he did, which neither of the men seemed to mind. One even propositioned to be patted again taking position against the wall of the club with his hands up on the stony surface. Ass out and legs spread while the two other men took advantage of the offer to feel him up. Gage rolled his bike back into an empty curb spot— still just watching. His mouth watering to have some toy time, but he made no move to join them or venture closer to the club.

"Hmm-hmm-hmm-hmm-mmm— man, oh, man. You look edible." A low barbering growl of a voice came up behind him, "Come inside, pretty baby, and I will ride you all night."

Gage twisted just as the arriving admirer, trailed by two comrades, stepped up to feel out one of Gage's arms still held out as he gripped a handlebar. Gage didn't play back. *Why was he so tense?* The offer wasn't so bad. But Gage couldn't bring himself to let go of the handlebars. His admirer didn't seem to notice the lacking response, too enthralled with the amusement of eye candy just one of Gage's arms offered while the admiring bear still stroked over Gage's bicep and then his shoulder.

The clubber still taking some liberty with Gage's physique, was dressed for the part of offering club slut. A pair of jeans with Timberland boots. A leather harness that showed off the matching set of salt and pepper hair on his head, chest, and forearms. His face groomed to allow only a small amount of stubble. But more importantly was what he wore just above the harness. *He was collared.*

Neither of the two comrades with the man seemed to eye him with any sense of ownership, but someone somewhere obviously did. Either way, it was a deal breaker for Gage. Too rough for his liking and he didn't much care for playing with other people's toys. Not even on loaner nights.

The man finally wandered off, figuring Gage would catch up when he was good and ready. No need for lengthy ceremonies here. And still Gage didn't budge.

*The last time he'd been here was also his first.* A night of endless fucking and sucking, but the ending was anything but bliss. A night that shattered his existence and turned Gage inside out only to find his pockets were empty and shelves void of memorabilia.

He sat there on his hog, staring at the door to the club as men, by ones, by twos, by threes, slowly arrived, and made their way inside. All, but Gage.

A few looked his way. Some with hopeful glances. Others unsteady of Gage's hovering. Still, Gage couldn't bring himself to go in.

An unseen ghost stood at the front door of this one, one he wasn't ready to face. So, he turned away— started the bike back up— then kicked it into gear and drove off— for home.

# 4

Gage spent his second weekend in his new home emptying out the last of his boxes. He'd have let them sit a while longer, but dammit he couldn't remember precisely where he packed his router and fleshjack. Both urgently important to his personal needs right now.

The internet had finally gotten turned on, but the jack for it was in the living room and Gage liked being mobile; so, he was determined to unearth his router. His fleshjack was for another matter. One week of ogling over Boomer and Gage's dick was singing a hard-core case of blue balls, something fierce. He'd rubbed a few off in the shower each night, but he was ready for some serious cranking on his dick and maybe some porn to boot.

Saturday morning was devoted to giving his fat hog some rubbing love of her own, having pulled it out into the short driveway, and he went to work with some polish. His neighbor, Tyrese, and one of his buddies had been out riding and dropped by to talk bikes, then talk workouts in the gym which led them to talking about chicks and Gage silently envisioned the mancandy he got to enjoy back at the gym. The neighbor bonding ended with a promise to have his wife bring up some brownies since she was baking today, and Gage went inside to tackle some more boxes and the mancandy-dilemma he was itching on now.

Sometime that afternoon, around box nine, and still no luck, his neighbor Darlayne dropped by with a plate of brownies just as her husband had promised. She called it a housewarming present then invited him up for the block party coming up next weekend and handed over the pan of chocolate overload.

The brownies were way more carbs than he cared to have in one sitting but given the amount of frustration he was convinced he was enduring, he accepted, and for her pleasure, popped one in his mouth right in front of her.

"Ohh— mmmm— these are good—" he tried to respond while his mouth was still stuffed, and he happily shoveled in another of the bite-size cut treats.

"Glad they put a smile on your face, you looked like you needed one of those." She turned to head out, when her healthy round hip bumped into a stack of boxes and sent them keeling over. Second one down fell open and out slid his fleshjack along with a dozen other unrelated items. One look and Darlayne was tossing a palm up to block the view, "Oh my. Way too much TMI up in this place." She glanced over her shoulder back at him and laughed, more at his frozen level gaze he gave her so not to give away that he might be embarrassed.

"Thanks, I was looking for that." He rolled with it.

Now the embarrassment was hers, but she shook it off, "Don't forget the party next week." She waggled a finger at him then made her way through the jungle of remaining boxes and showed herself out.

He glanced down at the three boxes now spilled out. At least he and his fleshjack were reunited, but now he also had to clean up the mess when he hadn't planned any more housework than it took to find his toy.

He popped another brownie in his mouth, humming a tune as he chewed, and started picking up the spilled items and carrying them off towards their new designated areas.

Before long he was starting to feel pretty damn good. Like a weight of fog had been lifted from his thoughts and before he knew it, he'd not only put away the three spilled boxes of stuff but continued on emptying out box after box. It was as if with each item he put away, his life was coming together. Like the random items he'd collected over the years were in some way the atoms of his body and soul. The organizing manner in which they were each put into a proper place sent vibrations out that mirrored the destiny of his life to fall into place and—

*Woah*— he ordered his mindless idiocy to stop as he became surprisingly aware he was fucking high as a kitc.

He went over to the counter where the remaining brownies sat and picked one up and gave it a closer inspection. It looked just like any ordinary brownie. He brought it to his nose and sniffed— smelled like a brownie too. He twisted and glanced around, wondering if he was suspecting the wrong thing, but Gage didn't have stuff like that in his boxes. He got his high off the adrenaline from working out or having great sex— *Sex —yeah, sex sounded pretty damn good right about now.* He shoved the brownie in his mouth then grabbed his fleshjack and headed for the shower.

He cranked up the hot water, letting the bathroom fill with a heavy fog of steam as he stripped down, then stepped in, and adjusting the setting on the shower head to massage. He turned, letting the pulsating water hit on the back of his neck and over his massive shoulders. *Ohh that felt so damn good.*

His eyes closed, feeling his body waver a bit. It was awkward, but he was too high to fully care either. He poured out some shower gel in his palm, lathered it up, then spread it over his building rolls of muscle, corded with veins that popped out under the layer of his freckled skin. He watched his hands slide over the galaxy of orange freckles that covered every part of his body, including his pecker with just a few at the base. But enough it'd gotten him a few chuckles from surprised lovers. Even Michael had loved to play with them. *Michael.* It'd been too long since he thought about him. Certainly, coming back had been the cause for the unwanted stroll down memory lane. Though it hit a bruised center in him, and Gage forcibly dismissed the memory, refusing to let it spoil his *selfie* time.

He worked the soap into the small nest of brassy orange hair around the base of his cock. Not nearly as much hair as he liked, but it was something easily remedied by the men he was attracted to. He pushed a handful of suds under his balls to wash his undercarriage, pulling the sack up to fondle them in his palm further, while his free hand washed everywhere else.

It felt good, the heat of the water kneading over his back while his hand slid up to deliver rough caresses to his more sensitive spots. Like his nipples— *damn he loved having a man's beard scrubbing over them then suck on them. Perhaps give them a hard nip or two.* He pinched one to add to his playing.

After a good body lather, he made a few turns under the spray of water, rinsed, then grabbed the two-in-one, poured out a dime of the lotion and worked it into the spiked hair on his head. Hair maintenance was simple for him. He kept the sides buzzed pretty short and leaving enough length on top to give his would-be partner a little something to grab onto while he got his mouth fucked.

He dropped his head back, pulling up the image of a man in front of him. In Gage's head, *the fantasy was taller than even the average tall man. And enough girth, Gage wasn't sure he'd be able to get his arms all the way around the man when he held him. His fantasy man's chest and arms were covered in a nice soft winter coat of brown fur that felt good under the palms of Gage's hands while he envisioned himself now lathering up the man in his head.* There was no doubt the image in his head was that of Boomer. *The quiet giant stood there waiting for Gage to make the next move, to show him what they were going to do. Gage saw himself take Boomer's head by the back of his hair and pulled him down for a fierce kiss, feeling the wooly beard scrape over his chin as they remained locked in a tongue match that went on forever, because in his fantasies he didn't have to stop to breathe.*

"Oh, fuck yeah." Gage groaned out loud, dropping his hand to his cock and began to work it over with a slow twist of his wrist.

He used his hands on his body to simulate what he wanted Boomer to do. His eyes closed, seeing the vision almost as clearly as he was watching it on the tv. *Fuck. Whatever was in those brownies was some potent shit.*

He leaned back on the tiles and moved his hips until his cock was directly under the stream of water. The spiral of water hitting right over the glans, sending sudden knee jerking waves of stimulation so intense it almost hurt in a pleasurable way. He felt the coiling tension in his perineum then spreading up into his balls until they were drawn tight against his body, making his dick ache all the more to cum. He was getting close, but he didn't want a quickie. Not with this man and certainly not with the fantasy in his head.

With a bitter growl, Gage wrenched his fist from his shaft and turned off the water. He didn't even bother with a towel, and just head straight for his bedroom. The cooler air caught his skin sending his freckles to rise up like braille from the goose bumps. His fleshjack and the bottle of lube already lying on his bed, waiting for him. He paused at the bureau pulling out his Colt brand vibrating dildo and tossed it to the bed as well, then laid out in total surrender to his toys.

Gage slopped some lube onto his fingers and reached behind him, pulling his ass cheek aside and stretched his arms until he felt the sensitive skin of his hole and slowly pushed his finger in. It wasn't an easy reach for him, being limited by his muscular build, but he managed to loosen himself up, then worked in the dildo.

He let out a heavy sigh as he gently pumped it in and out until it breached the tight ring of muscle, then sank all the way in. He rolled to his back, using the mattress to keep it in place. And he squirmed his hips around, which in turn moved the vibrating cock around in his ass. "Oh, fuck yeah, it's been a while," he moaned then grabbed the fleshjack, squirted some lube in it, and then drew it over his cock that still jutted out from his body turned nearly red; he was so ready. "Oh Fuck!" He pivoted his hips up then down into the mattress, working his ass and cock at the same time. All while in his head, he and Boomer were going at it. His free hand roamed over his abs and up over his chest to tweak a nipple. He squirmed and rolled, changing up the angles of his toys and tightened the muscles in his ass; working the vibe inside him until he found the right angle that got it to press against his *prostie* and that was all it took. Just that added pressure in the right angle and Gage's body tensed, nearly sending him jackknifing up in the bed. He cried out some incomprehensible word that trailed into a chain of lock jaw growling.

"F-f-f-f-fuuuck!" He finally managed to push a real word out as the last of his release pumped out of his cock, filling up the fleshjack and then spilling back out over his groin and balls.

When it was over, he collapsed a moment, surrendering to the post coital bliss, and letting the fleshjack slide off on its own to drop to the bed. The Colt still pulsed in his ass, sparking a few after quakes until he summoned up enough energy to role to his side and pull it out.

He let out a heavy sigh, giving over to the spaced-out feeling from his release, letting the vibrator fall from his hand, and crash to the floor, not caring. He'd clean up— *later.*

He didn't want to move anymore. *Fuck, a good selfie fix had been what he needed.* Not the same as having the real thing, but he felt better, nonetheless.

Gage just laid there sprawled out over the bed, completely spent, and still super high. He stared up at the ceiling, seeing the darkness swirl about, but not in a way to say he was hallucinating, all the visions were safely still in his head. *One being of Boomer zonked out beside him. His heavy arm slung across Gage's chest practically pinning him to the bed with its sheer mass A deep breath rumbled in the man's chest like a hibernating teddy bear.* Gage liked the idea of that. *And Boomer's quietness certainly made him seem like he'd make a perfect Teddy Bear.*

He finally closed his eyes, letting the floating feeling of the high carrying him off to slumber. But just as he felt like he had drifted off, his eyes sprung open and stared back up at the ceiling.

*Dammit— I'm hungry.*

Forty minutes later, Gage found himself standing at the front door of his home, with a hard scowl on his face over the red taillights of the pizza delivery kid already halfway down the street. He glanced at the open pizza box balanced on his hand and at the sacrilegious abused form of what should have been a pepperoni and mushroom pizza. He stared at the alien forms on the pizza, his lip curling up in dissatisfaction. "Who the hell puts pineapple, ham, artichokes, and banana peppers on a pizza?" He growled at it. The sad part was the dope induced munchies were kicking up a hard battle in his belly and laying siege on his will power to say: *Hell, no I won't go* in his mind. "Dammit, I'm hungry." He muttered realizing he'd just lost the war and rcached in pulling one of the slices free and folded it over in one hand. He sniffed at it speculatively, then closed his eyes and shoved it in for a full bite. *All or nothing.*

# 5

Sometime that following afternoon, Gage got up and took a long shower to clear the cobwebs that had taken up residence in his head. "Oooh-uuugh." He groaned, dunking his head under the hot shower, "What the fuck was in those brownies?"

After discovering he didn't have anything appealing in the fridge for a hangover he decided to ride up to the store. Maybe Darlayne would be working evenings and she could explain to him this odd *welcome to the neighborhood* tradition.

"Damn, I am starved for carbs right now," he grumbled as he went down one aisle then the next grabbing up bacon, eggs, bread, three different jams, oatmeal, several lunch meats, and cheeses. On the next aisle he picked out two bags of chips, a bag of beef jerky, and a package of double stuffed Oreos before toting it all up to the register.

Darlayne was already waiting on him, with a cringing grin that had apology written all over it.

"Oooo, you okay?" she asked when it was finally his turn in line to get rung up.

"My head is pounding, and my fridge wasn't prepared for a man my size to suddenly have an appetite explosion. Seems you weren't the only one swapping deliveries, last night the pizza guy delivered someone else's pizza to me. I was so high and hungry, I ended up eating a pizza with some of the strangest toppings on it." He shook his head with a chuckle, "Ate every last bite too."

She did what she could to stifle her laugh and if it weren't for her eyes still begging for forgiveness some people might not have found it as humorous as she did. But he couldn't bring himself to feel offended that she was definitely laughing at him.

"I am really sorry; I got the trays mixed up somehow. I don't usually make that mistake. But I hope you're okay. It wasn't intentional."

"What was in them, if you don't mind me asking?"

"Pot." She wrinkled up her nose. "Edna Harris, who lives right behind me, has terminal cancer. Her doctor gives it to her to keep her comfortable. It's ionized hydro, the good stuff. But Edna doesn't like to smoke it, makes her house smell like a skunk's mating convention. So, I make the brownies for her every other week," Darlayne explained as she rang up his groceries then bagged them up.

"Guess I should give you some money then to help get that replaced?" Gage was ready to drop a few extra bills if it would help.

"Oh." She waved her hand down, "I'll get one of the street kids to make a donation. Edna's been around since most of these gangsters was in diapers. And while they might be heading in the wrong direction, they aren't all soured inside-out. I'm just glad you're not mad at me." She pushed the brown paper bags towards him, then paused looking up at him, wincing. "You aren't, are you?"

Gage thought about it and realized he wasn't really. He wasn't keen on getting high, but it was the best selfie fun he'd had in some time. "Nah, but next time you're baking, you owe me a pumpkin pie. Hold the garnish."

She smiled warmly. "You're on. One pumpkin pie, hold the ganja."

# 6

That Monday, Gage went into work early, just so he could work off some of the extra food he'd put down after his brownie mishap. Not even the remaining boxes and a twenty-four-dollar shelf kit from the local hardware store had come close to burning off all that junk food. The only thing that was going to work the ton of calories and carbs he'd consumed Saturday night and into Sunday was maybe one of those fantasies he'd drummed up in his head about breaking in the new mattress. Like the one with Boomer on his back with his hairy legs up in the air. Or, realistically, Gage getting his ass in the gym and working it off the right way. Though, he wouldn't turn down a proposition from Boomer if he ever got the chance either.

Within an hour, Gage had already run the gauntlet, down the line of nautilus equipment. He liked how everything was arranged; twenty-one variable systems lined up and then back down creating a twenty-one full body work out system to warm up with. Starting with legs, then arms, back to legs and then ending with the core. He had a little more time left before he needed to clean up for his first appointment, so he decided to do some dead weights and test his threshold on the bench press. He was just laying back after adding another plate to each end of his press-bar when the very body that'd been preoccupying his thoughts all weekend was standing right at his head.

Gage looked up to find Boomer towering over him, looking down. "Boomer." Gage hardly reached five-ten, so even standing, Boomer's six-eight was a good jump over his head. However, looking up from the perspective of laying back, Boomer seemed as tall as the 30 Hudson Street building.

"You should always have a spotter."

"You offering?" Gage asked, knowing full well anyone of the guys already in the gym would have stepped over to help had Gage buckled. So, Boomer coming up to suggest it may have been a ploy for other things. Gage liked to think so at least.

He took in the full view of Boomer. He was wearing the usual option of gym pants rather than jeans today, and the crisp white t-shirt hugged Boomer's body in all the right ways that not even the shirt's large screen print of a sketched-out gray-n-white kitten could muster up. Gage had never been provided with a gratuitous show of Boomer skin before, but what he did get to see was heavily dusted in hair, a dark shade of brown, which Gage had long since determined would go rather nicely with his own pumpkin-colored freckles.

The giant nodded slightly then held a handout to be on the ready then crooked his fingers to say *let's go.*

Gage adjusted his grip, so the bar sat more on the heel of his hand rather than towards his fingers to proposition the weight polar to his wrist rather than his hand. He sucked in a deep breath then released the weighted press bar from its hooks and slowly brought it down to his chest mimicked by the slow steady breath he blew from his lips in a slight pucker. He sucked in another deep breath to gather up the inertia to press, but what he got instead was a deep smell of the man standing just inches from his head. *Fuck, Boomer smelled good.*

Gage shook the thoughts from his head, sucked in another tantalizing breath then pressed the weight bar up. He felt the muscles of his triceps, pectorals, and deltoids strain towards his goal. His determination transferred to the drive in his arms to keep pushing until his elbows bumped into the *Finish*, straight over his shoulders. He held the weight steady a moment then slowly brought it back down to his *Start*.

Having Boomer to spot him was more a distraction than it was a help. He felt his arms shake more than they should as he let his eyes wander to get the close-up glimpse of the man's thighs. *Oh, fuck yeah.* Big thick racks of grade-A beef and Gage could just make out the imprint of the bull-sized dick hanging down the left leg of Boomer's pants.

Gage made a hard inhaled and pressed again, drawing up more images in his head with Boomer. He saw Boomer pulling that cock out to give him a show if he bench-pressed just one more. Bench two and Boomer offered to lay that piece of meat over

Gage's face and slap it across his chin. Fuck pressing, Gage saw himself reaching up taking Boomer's hips and drawing the man down until his cock slipped into Gage's mouth and he sucked it all the way down until Boomer's sack was nestled over Gage's nose where he could breathe in all that Teddy Bear musk. "Fuck yeah, I could suck you down right now."

Gage froze, his arms locked in the *Finish* straight over his head bearing the weight of six 45lbs iron plates per side. A total scale of 620lbs. He pitched his arms beyond his shoulders and let the bar return into the holders, "Damn. I said that out loud, didn't I?"

Boomer didn't say a word, instead his eyes flickered to something else at Gage's feet. He looked and there was Skye gawping at him. Gage bolted up, slamming his forehead on the weight bar which sent him right back down to the bench, "Skye." He exclaimed rubbing his forehead and trying once more to sit up, albeit more carefully this time. "You're early."

She shrugged and nodded indifferently. "Teacher's workday."

Gage glanced over his shoulder, but Boomer had already wandered off, leaving Gage without the benefit of even knowing what kind of reaction Boomer had to his forward remark.

"Soooo— are you really wanting to suck Mr. Boomer's, yanno, his dick?"

Gage snapped around and gave her a surprised look, he was about to say something about her choice definition of bodily parts, but clamped his mouth shut, reminding himself she was still in high school *and* a minor. "Just for that, you can do fifty lunges down the strip."

"Tuh!" she spat.

"And another ten for that." He cracked his neck one way then the next, then stretched his arms out and around behind him before pushing up to his feet to lead his teen tantrum to the back where the heavier weights awaited her. "If you're going to be on an Olympic team, you need to learn to watch your language, as they have a strict moral code of ethics and etiquette."

"But you were the one saying you wanted to suck him down where everyone could hear you."

Gage stopped and glanced at her a moment. He could say he wasn't the one trying out for the

Olympics, but he also knew firsthand the *do as I say not as I do* wasn't going to teach her anything. "Fair enough." And he grabbed a dumb bell in each hand then right alongside her he did fifty lunges down the strip. The odd thing was when they got done, Boomer was at the end with a water and hand towel for each of them. A faint smile seemed to reflect from his eyes at Gage, then as always Boomer turned and walked away before anything more could pass between them.

They spent the afternoon working on her form much to her fuss, doing dead lifts with little more than fifty pounds on her bar whereas the bar alone only added another twenty-five pounds to the total weight. Strength-wise the lightweight bar was nothing compared to what she could lift, but this was where he taught them best how to control the movement of the weight and not the other way around. Her first couple of lifts resulted in her swinging the bar up too fast and unable to break the momentum of the lift. So, Skye and the bar went flipping backwards onto the mat.

"See there. This is why we are working on your form."

'It's too light. It just flies up because I'm used to three times more than this!" she shouted at him with little more than her ego bruised from the fall. "It's too easy."

"Ah, if it's so easy, then why did it send you to your ass, huh?" He pulled her back onto her mark, then set the bar in front of her. He knelt down in front of her this time, crooking a finger for her to get into her squatting position. He gripped her wrists as she wrapped her fingers around the bar, then he looked her dead in the eyes. "Don't anticipate your weight. Know it. Don't plan to react to the movement, control it. If twenty-two kilograms can send you over just by its velocity, then what's to stop a hundred and forty-three kilos?"

He released her arms and scooted back but didn't take his eyes from hers; eyes that were as cool as a pitcher of ice water. Never before had he met or seen a black person with blue eyes that didn't come from contacts. She was light skinned and her eyes had a slight angle to them, like she had some Asian, or some Pacific Islander ethnicity in her or something. But those blue eyes he couldn't figure out at all. However, they watched him, saw what he told her and that was good.

"Know what moves you're going to make and what ones you won't allow. When you lift, lift straight up for the sky, not up and over. That's the key, Skye. Lift for the sky, not swing." He stood this time, but rather than take a full step back to be clear of the bar, he stood his ground. If she hit him, then her form was wrong. And they would do it over and over again until she stopped hitting him in the lift. "See what you're going to do in your head. Visualize the motion from your *Start* and to your *Finish*. When you know how you are going to finish it, that's when you do it."

He waited— watching her eyes flicker as they pictured something only she could see. She licked her lips, rolling them in, in a mock grimace, then curled her fingers around the bar. The muscles in her arms drew taut then— up— her legs drove her body up in an explosive hip and knee extension, hefting the bar with her. Her back contorted into a less than normal strained arch at the point of full body extension, then dropped under the bar as her arms snapped it up and over her head. Her body core returning to its start. Only, this time, the weighted bar stopped, and she maintained a steady balanced position in her squat. She followed up with a pushed-to-standing, keeping her arms locked out, high overhead where she held it for the five count. She released the bar, letting gravity take it to the ground, and it bounced to a stop on the mat between them. The reward was having her look up at him with a proud grin. Not only had she done it, she had felt the difference. And the bar never glanced his body.

"Well done. Now let's see you do it again."

They spent her last thirty minutes working on her *Snatch* lifts, then her *Clean & Jerks*, slowly adding a little more weight back into her bar.

Next in Gage's day were Mitch and Mike. Mike was easy enough to work with, but Mitch still had a chip on his shoulder about still working on basic form.

"I've been going to gyms since I was fifteen and been competing for the last 6 years. I don't need you coming in here and telling me I'm doing it wrong, and I am sick of your shit!" Mitch finally burst out, throwing his towel down, "Come on, Mike. Time to find a new gym."

Gage never took the yelling very serious, just another temper tantrum. All ego, all for show and no real wounds from hard work, yet. "How many times you tear out your right rotator cuff last year?" Gage asked, gathering up stray items of gear to put back on their holding hooks with hardly a glance at the man who came to a complete stall in his exit. It was no guess on Gage's part that the man had. The way he was pitching to one side using his right arm to favor his left only succeeded in putting his shoulders out of alignment at the precise moment he launched his javelin lift. With his shoulder misaligned for a full rotation it was going to tear out his cuff every time.

"Twice." Mitch turned and gave him a surprised look.

"At some point you injured your left shoulder. That set you down the path of compensating— putting an unbalanced strain on your right, to favor it ever since. Even if your left arm isn't giving you any trouble you've trained into the bad habit and now you keep tearing it up your right no matter how many times you injure it. Time to balance your shoulders and take that pivot out of your shoulders in your lifts." Gage gave Mike a weary glance, noting he'd gotten his attention, "If you want to survive this season's Strongman you might want to stay or you can do it your way, and your doctor will have to do surgery next time around. Then all those years of doing it your way won't have done you a damn bit of good. Once you go under the knife, your competition days will be over." Gage hung the straps back up on the hangers and just waited. Mitch took one look at his twin and folded, giving Gage *the nod,* consenting he would shut up and learn.

After the twins, Gage had some time, Jamal was usually his next for the day, but was out on an away game, so that gave Gage a free hour. Which he used to put together a shopping list of hardware he needed to customize some of the equipment for his athletes.

"Know where I can find a decent hardware store around here? Need to pick up a few things to make some modifications for these guys." Gage asked as he brought up his list to the counter where Boomer was going through some paperwork.

The mountain-sized man reached under the counter then pulled out a catalog and handed it over. "We're not that run down. Just be sure you buy shit that lasts instead of shit that looks cool in the pictures."

Gage looked down seeing Boomer had handed him a catalog. He stayed right there flipping through the pages, looking up the parts he needed while taking advantage of the opportune moment to admire Boomer's body. And he took his sweet time doing it too, before handing his list of part's numbers to Boomer to approve. Gage wondered if Boomer would comment on what had happened earlier, but Boomer said nothing. The most he got was Boomer's approval for handling the twins as he did.

"Say, you think Schiller will approve some money to have a physical therapist come in here once a week to see a couple of the guys, like Mitch and Skye, as needed? I can look around, find a couple of options that have the skills I am looking for, and get their fees from them before bringing it to him."

Boomer sucked in a deep breath and glanced up from his paperwork at Gage and scratched at his beard thoughtfully, "Make sure at least one candidate is local. Like, lives local. He'll look at it more seriously that way," he commented, then went back to his paperwork and started checking things off with a pencil. "Oh, by the way, make sure when you come in, you park on the street from now on, not on the sidewalk."

Gage frowned, but he hadn't forgotten what Boomer had done to the one guy's Honda and Gage sure as hell didn't want the same to happen to his bike.

"Yeah, alright, just trying to keep it safe. It's the only thing of value I have."

"No worries. I took care of that for you."

"What do you mean?" Gage quizzed him.

Boomer only nodded his head towards the door and Gage went out to check. Right there in front, directly behind the handicap spot was a space marked out in bright red painted lines. A space marked just large enough for Gage's motorcycle to park in. Stenciled on the sidewalk, next to it, the words: GYM STAFF ONLY.

Gage quickly stepped back in, "You did that for me?" he asked, transferring from the bright outdoors to the dark insides of the gym, but when his eyes adjusted, he saw Boomer was already disappearing into his office. The door swinging closed with a soft click.

# 7

Months went by and Gage had found very little variation to the routines of the gym, as well as very little bonding. Boomer was almost always keeping himself at arm's length when it came to personal interaction. No matter how often they spoke or even the occasional awkward collision in and out of the locker room. A few of those were even deliberate on Gage's part. However, for Boomer, Gage's attempts to open the door of opportunity between them either went over the man's head or had Boomer back stepping quickly. None had fruited into anything beyond a few glancing touches.

Lunch was about the extent of their time sharing. Boomer always brought in lunch with enough to share. On rare occasions Schiller joined them before he left for the day.

As it turned out, Gage had finally learned the identities of Charlie and Roberta. They were Schiller's partners. Roberta being another man and Charlie was short for Charlene. The three had been together in a polyamorous threesome for going on twenty years. In fact, they were going to be celebrating an anniversary soon. Whether that meant a party or not, Gage couldn't say. And neither did Schiller.

Where Gage had hoped for something, he'd been unable to get even the first grasp on in his new start on life— he'd found nothing. Once more he was just a cog in the wheel, and he was beginning to think it was time to start looking elsewhere. He didn't want to waste more years without a connection like he did in LA. He wasn't getting any younger, but he sure as hell was aware he *was* getting lonelier.

Another Friday rolled around, which seemed to be the highlight of his weeks here. The polishing crew were in earlier this time. It was movie night for the new *Star Trek* release and the gang wanted to be finished and have time to get ready for opening night.

Joshua had become Gage's hug buddy, always hanging nearby to talk and hug him again. Today Joshua was wearing a *Star Wars* storm trooper mask in preparation for the night's movie adventure. Of course, no amount of telling him he was wearing the wrong mask deterred his enthusiasm. As it turned out, Joshua lectured, with a rather lengthy line of infinite possibilities that had Gage, and several other guys listening in. Convinced that somehow in *Star Trek 5*, when the evil being that had been mistaken as God had been accidently set loose and had then fled into another galaxy, the escaped evil villain became the evil chancellor who started the *Empire Strikes Back*. That's when the mistaken god proclaimed himself the Dark Lord of the Sith in the *Star Wars* franchise.

*It had been far more convincing when Joshua told it.*

Abi was another one Gage had gotten to know a bit. She was older than most of them, but her childlike playfulness was in step with the others. She had thin blonde hair, cut in a clean straight line along her shoulders and she often wore an oversized bow to keep it out of her eyes.

Abi had been the woman who apparently hid the super suit from all the guys, which was their regular shouting game anytime she came to visit. She also had an apparent crush on Boomer. *Who could blame her?* In fact, she was the only one out of the group that would sometimes come in on non-work-team days alone, visiting Boomer, and always cheering the guys on to work harder.

At the moment, she was up front in a battle of *yes/no* wits of God knows what with Boomer. A comedy in and of itself from Gage's audience-like perception; to see this plump round woman, who he doubted tipped a few inches over five feet, shouting a defiant *yes* up at the well-over six-pushing-seven-foot giant of fuzziness who countered with a stern *no,* following it with an audible grumble and growl at the next defiant *yes.*

Gage would have moved in for a closer seat, but he was otherwise preoccupied, tolerating Joshua's usual excessive curiosity about Gage's freckles. Joshua had since learned that Gage had far too many freckles to play connect the dot, but today, with the *Star Trek* theme in the air, Joshua had changed his tune and was now tracing out star constellations with a marker on Gage's arm. Gage wasn't any know-it-all on stars, but he was pretty sure Joshua had drawn several accurately.

Before Joshua had finished, Abi had abandoned the argument with Boomer and came up to join them. She looked tired today, the way the dark circles under her eyes shadowed her otherwise usual sweet glowing expressions. She inched in closer, admiring Joshua's constellation mapping and then, out of nowhere, she licked Gage's non-star-mapped arm.

Gage just looked at her with a blank expression. Abi, however, grinned ear to ear up at him as if she'd just licked a tree at Willie Wonka's chocolate factory, which seemed to brush away the strangely tired look in her eyes, then she dashed off before he could ask why.

"Okay, gang!" The team's driver called out from the front door, "Time to go. We don't want to be late for the movie." And like ants the crew milled out with a buzz of excitement.

And just in time too, Skye had just walked in, and the drill Gage had planned for today wasn't going to be pleasant. Something Gage wouldn't want their Friday team to witness. But for Skye, it was necessary.

As Gage had learned, Skye's school was poor like most schools around here were. They didn't have the budget or staff to support most sports either. How they managed was that she and a handful of others from various schools shared one coach who had them all congregate at one of the more centrally located schools. At competitions, they went together as a district team. But the equipment afforded by any of the schools didn't come close to their athletes' capabilities. That's where Gage came in. Though he was a secondary trainer, it was him and this gym that made her reach her limits then push them.

Her school coach had actually paid Gage a visit a couple of weeks ago. Skye had barely been making the points at the meets to keep her in the running. Then just two weeks ago when the scouts dropped in on one of the meets to have a look, Skye had come up dead last, making little impression on those who had the power to invite her to try for the Olympic team. Since then, Gage had her coming in every day, Monday through Friday. Leg day, arm day, core, form day, and drill day and all of them being lift days. She was hitting a ceiling within herself and going no further. However, Gage was determined to push her to break that limit today.

He started her off with her warmups and then straight to the Snatches. Working up to her limit in just ten sets. The moment he added another ten pounds, Skye buckled. He switched her over to the Smith Machine and loaded it up with 300lbs of weight. She needed to reach a goal to top 332lbs on the Clean & Jerk, but it was her legs not following up on the drive, so repetition on some squats would hopefully do her some good. The Smithie also forced her to rework her dips, allowing herself to sit deeper, challenging her body to drive harder for the bench. With each set of five benches she accomplished, Gage added ten more to her bar. But when her load was at 340lbs, she crushed two-thirds the way up.

"You gotta push, baby girl. You need to stop hitting your head on that ceiling."

"I'm trying," she fussed, while rubbing the burn from the triceps under her arms.

"No. You're just doing what you have already done. Thing is, you're not doing anything greater than the others. You can't just match them; you have to beat them."

"I'm trying, okay!" she shouted. "But it's just seems like no matter what I do, I can't get ahead."

"Then it's time you learned to push past your give-ups."

Skye spun at him with a hot glare. "I haven't been giving up!"

"Skye, you stop the second you're head hits that top."

"I don't know what you're talking about!"

Gage nodded. He glanced around, seeing that some of the others were looking their way.

To an outsider it might have sounded like Gage just told her *her good* wasn't good enough. And in a way he had, but not to tear her down. She needed a push and a damn hard one.

He waved her to follow, and he headed down along the far wall to the sled and toe strip that was designed specifically for the Strongman competitors. He motioned for her to grab a weight and together they began mounting plates onto the sled as he talked. "There's a thing called the dead man's crawl.

The military use it to train soldiers. They crawl through some brutal obstacle courses with weighted backpack on. Some football coaches use it, making players carry a teammate on their back and crawl on hands and feet down the hundred-yard line.

"So?"

"So, today, you're going to do your own dead man's crawl."

Skye just looked at him with a fair amount of *fuck you* mixed with trepidation. She had long since stopped asking why he made her do things that didn't seem related to her goal, only to find that every muscle he made her work actually did help in one way or another. He'd slowly manipulated her training over the months that had improved her lifts in the end. Today he hoped to train her spirit.

Gage watched as Skye looked at him and then down the length of the strip. It was three-and-a-half-foot wide aisle that ran from the front of the gym all the way down to the very back, stopping just shy of the boxing ring. The surface had been given a gritty surface by adding sand to the paint to give the trainers' better grip.

She glanced back at him. "But it's only a hundred feet or so."

"A hundred and twenty-one to be exact."

"So, what's the point?"

Gage picked up a sandbag and added it to the sled's weight. "You're going to be dragging more weight than any of those football players or soldiers have ever had to carry a day in their life." He caught the nervous swallow and some of that soft malt skin color seemed to drain away from her face. "You can do this, Skye. You have it in you to do this. You've just never pushed your boundaries."

She glanced once more down the strip and to the few guys that had started to take notice and she nodded. If not all that confidently.

Gage waved her to take a spot in front of the sled, and he helped wrap the harness around her. Two well-padded harness straps, about two and half inches wide, looped over her shoulders and clipped at the center of her back to a tether. He snapped the buckle across her chest which made sure the straps didn't slip, then walked her out until the tether between her and the sled was stretched.

Skye leaned forward into position, letting the tether became tight and held her hovering over the floor in a mid-air lunge.

Gage looked her dead in the eyes just as he always did, met the person inside, and spoke to her soul. "Don't Quit." Then he reached out, placing a bandana around her eyes, and tied it at the back of her head.

"Blindfolded?"

"Yep. It's a straight line. You can do this." He stepped back, "GO, SKYE!"

Skye lunged for him, taking the sled off its fixed spot right away. She leaned full on into the harness until her fingers nearly hovered over the floor and she took another step then another. Her body straining with each step that dragged over a thousand pounds of iron and sand behind her. Ten steps and she began to lean closer to the floor and she dropped her knees.

"Keep your knees up off the ground. Keep going. You're doing good."

"It's heavy!" She pushed and took two more steps.

"I know its heavy, but you keep going. Don't quit! You can do this!"

"Ugh," she cried out but took another step.

"Why do you do what you do if you're not going to keep going? Don't quit now. You're doing good. You can do this, but don't quit," Gage carried on, never letting his prodding stall in her head or efforts. Keeping the driving energy pounding out like a war drum to push her.

Skye pushed and stepped— pushed and stepped— exertion and strain— until her knees dropped to the floor again.

"Get your knees up. Hands and feet only."

She repositioned so her palms gripped the strip in front of her, her hips high up in the air, and her feet digging into the floor.

"You want to make it to the games. Now use it for your drive to keep going. Just like when you control your weights, don't let your body trick you into thinking you can't do this. Don't let the weakness control you. Be in control of your destiny and keep going!"

She let out a growl and reached out and took another step and then another— and another. The strain of the sled's weight bearing evidence in every straining muscle of her body and more so in the tension that built in her face. Defeat and determination warring around in her head behind her eyes. But Gage's pushing convinced her to win this. The doubt derailed in her expression, and she shoved all her strength into the harness that connected her to the weight trying to hold her back. The sled began to move down the strip like there was nothing that could possibly get in her way. The guys in the gym all gathered around. Some began to cheer her on and she reached and stepped— again— and again.

She made it ten— fifteen— more steps before she cried out, "It Burns!" And the counterproductive thought slowed her next reach.

She was almost to the halfway mark. But halfway wasn't enough. She had to finish. Win or lose, she had to finish— no matter what. Just never quit. But Gage could see she was almost at that line where she was going to give herself permission to stop. "You keep going, now isn't the time to stop. You keep going."

She reached, but that next step didn't happen as the harness and the weight of the sled pulled her back. "I can't."

Gage stayed alongside her with every step. His verbal commands level to her ear to drum out any negative ideas. "Yes, you can! You keep going! Don't Quit. Don't Quit! You keep going!" Gage started shouting over her fatalist comments, determined to overrule even tomorrow's thoughts in her head. Driving her relentlessly to keep at it.

Skye lunged again, but her effort was half as much and once more she failed to make another step.

"Give it your all! Don't quit on me!"

"Uuuurgh! I can't! It's too heavy!" Her head hung low, broadcasting her protests to the floor.

"Yes, you can! You keep going!"

She lunged and managed another step and then another. They were slower, but she was moving again, and Gage began shouting at her more.

"THIRTY MORE STEPS! KEEP GOING! KEEP GOING, SKYE! DON'T QUIT!"

She began to cry, but she still took another step, "Its burning!"

"THEN LET IT BURN! BUT YOU KEEP GOING!" He kept alongside her with each agonizing step, "DON'T QUIT! DON'T YOU QUIT, SKYE!"

"But I can't!" she nearly sobbed.

"Hey man, lay off her. She can't do it," someone behind Gage called out.

"Don't you listen to them, Skye! They don't have to live with the results if you quit now! You keep going!"

"I can't!"

"YES, YOU CAN! YOU KEEP GOING!" he bellowed at her, not letting anyone tear into the mojo he ensued in her, "DON'T CRY TO QUIT, CRY TO KEEP GOING! YOU ALREADY KNOW WHAT IT'S LIKE TO NOT GET THERE! NOW IS THE TIME TO CHANGE THAT! SO, YOU KEEP GOING! YOU LOOK DEEP DOWN INSIDE YOU AND YOU FIND THAT STRENGTH YOU NEED! YOU FIND THAT ENERGY AND YOU DON'T STOP!"

"AHHH! I hate YOU!" she screamed at him, pressing her body into the harness.

"Good! USE IT! But don't you quit on me! Come on, Skye! Pull! Keep going!"

And suddenly Skye found what she needed and lunged forward— the sled moved once again and she reached and stepped, reached and stepped.

Ten feet—

Twenty feet—

Twenty-five—

"That's it! Keep going! Keep going! Just 20 more steps! Keep going! You're almost there! Keep going! Don't quit!"

Reach and step— her body straining while her arms reached blindly out in front of her, and her legs followed through with another step. She cried and shouted right back at him, but the sled didn't stop moving this time.

Reach and step—

Reach and step—

"Almost there! Almost there! Ten more steps! Just ten more! Don't quit! Just a little further!!"

The harness held in the next step, and she stilled in mid-effort. Her face contorted behind the bandana over her eyes, teeth gritted in agony even as tears wet her cheeks and chin. "AHHHHG! I can't! I can't do it anymore!" she cried out, but still she leaned forward more and managed to take another step then reached again. The sled moving with her.

"THAT'S IT, SKYE! KEEP GOING! YOU'RE DOING IT!"

She made one last lunge then fell to the floor and gave out. "I'm sorry! I can't do it. I can't go any further," she sobbed face down in the floor. "I'm out of strength."

Gage knelt down beside her, taking her shoulder to roll over and pulled the bandana from her eyes, "You already made it, baby girl," he said proudly and as she looked to see what he and all the others did, she saw she had more than just crossed the line at the end of the strip, she was laying a full length of her body past it.

For all the crying about not having any more energy there was a little bit left as she sprang up, wrapping her arms around his neck in an exhausted hug.

The gym was quiet now save for the few still in the back at the boxing ring. Everyone else had already taken off for their weekend plans. Gage was up front with Boomer, leaning back in one of the metal folding chairs with the back rested against the wall, downing a bottle of water after some work out time of his own. His attention now focused, enjoying the view of Boomer's arms propped up on the counter while he worked the books for the week's intake and expenses.

"You don't think you pushed her too hard?" Boomer asked, showing little if any hint of what he was actually thinking or feeling on the matter.

"She desperately needed to top some more weight."

"How much more?"

"If her goal is to make the Olympic team, she has to be able to beat the gold medalist. Every Olympic Game and World Youth Championship, the girls have been getting stronger. Skye can't go into that just matching what they did four years ago. She has to go in planning to top whatever gain they are working towards for the next one."

Boomer stopped what he was doing and looked at him, "What are we talking about here?"

"Last year's WYC, the Snatch was 132 kg and the Clean & Jerk was 151kg with a total weight point of 272kg. The last Olympic Games the weights were 117 and 145. So, she has to set her goals to top last year's points by 6kg if she wants to make the final cut."

Boomer shook his head. "She's not there yet. She's lifting almost eight, ten grams under that."

"Yes, she is. That's what today was about. A different perspective to push the threshold and go beyond her comfort zone. Winning doesn't happen in the safe zone. She's had it in her. She just hasn't been pushed to do it."

"I hope you're right. Because, if you're wrong and she doesn't get the invite to try for the team, school coach is dropping her."

"She'll find out Monday then. Because if she doesn't push past her limits and at least match the Olympic game weights in next week's regionals, she won't make those needed extra points to catch anyone's attention anyways."

Boomer let out a thoughtful sigh, then looked back at Gage from over his shoulder. "I saw you giving her something before she left. What was it?"

Gage grinned more to himself than anything and finished off the last of his water before answering, "I little bit of mojo power."

# 8

Monday rolled around slow as molasses, and Gage found himself in an odd sort. Somewhere, seven states away, Skye would be competing today. And whether she won or not, someone else would take the credit or shit-can her for it.

Gage, however, had spent the weekend staring at those empty shelves he'd built that one night while high as a kite. Shelves he hadn't added one damn thing to.

In LA, he had a similar set of shelves. Only they were filled with framed photos of pumped up, oiled out guys posing next to monstrously tall trophies. He even had a few mock copies of those trophies, compliments of the gym for a job well done. When Gage left LA, he left them too. Not one of those pictures or trophies meant a damn thing to him. That thought train led Gage to the whys he'd gone out to LA in the first place. *A new start,* he said.

Escape the loss of a relationship that hadn't filled all the corners of his being as a whole. Yet, it was what he'd had, all up until Michael was killed in the car crash. Seven years went by and while he'd never used Michael as an excuse to avoid another commitment, one never was offered either. That too had remained meaningless and untouched.

Now here he was back at the beginning and still nothing to show for it all. He hadn't even gotten the first photo in five months at the gym to put on his shelf. A cold reminder he hadn't managed to accomplish a damn thing. Much like anything else. *Like Boomer.*

Gage couldn't say that his approaches had failed, because in reality, Boomer had thwarted every opportunity of Gage getting a chance to even make any kind of pass or invite for a night out to the quiet giant. It was like he was cock block cursed or something. The worst was, Gage liked it here. Always had. But something was keeping him from setting roots, so he figured it was time to say goodbye.

Schiller wasn't none too pleased about the news either. Had the man put up a fight about it, Gage might have relented and stuck it out a little longer, but Schiller didn't push him and that was Gage's signal that this wasn't the place for him. The right one would push him to stick it out. *One more step! Keep going and don't quit! Don't quit!*

The day was quiet without Skye to fuss at every work out. No visit from Abi. Mitch and Mike had stopped fighting and started working, always adding one more to the rep, and Jamal was out on another game. So, Gage spent a better part of the day just going through all the equipment, fixing and adjusting so that everything would be in top shape when he fulfilled his two-week notice.

Seven o'clock dragged in and Gage didn't even look up to watch Boomer leave. *What was the point?*

"Hey, put all that down and let's go."

Gage looked up from the leg press he was making adjustments on to see Boomer at the door looking back at him, his finger on the light switch."

"I have to clean up."

"Never mind all that. If we hurry, we might catch it."

"Catch what?" Gage called out a little aggravated.

"Just drop what you're doing and come with me. That's an order."

Gage followed behind Boomer's truck as they drove through town, heading over to the south side. He had half a mind to abandon Boomer, but his words *that's an order,* tumbling in the back of Gage's head, had sounded damn sexy and, well, Gage hadn't heard anything even remotely demanding as that from the man since they'd met. So, Gage was curious as to what was up. Even if he was still agitated by it as well.

When they arrived at the destination, Boomer waved Gage to squeeze his bike past the multitude of cars that crowded in the driveway, front yard, and curbside. And then they both headed into the mystery home.

"YAY!" a woman shouted amidst the crowd of people, "They made it! They made it!" A well rounded and robust heavy-set woman came bounding their way. A beer in each hand, held high over her head so as not to lose them by any accidental collision while enroute through the crowd of guests in the living room. And once she arrived, it was Gage who got the first hug.

The woman then pushed the beers on them, one into Gage's hand, and the other into Boomer's, then reached up grabbing Gage's face and pulled him down for an awkward kiss before swinging her arms wide to receive a hug from Boomer, who willing bent down to deliver.

"I'm Lenora." She turned back to Gage. "I'm Skye's momma." Her smile was as big and as wide as any that no one'd ever guess they'd never met.

Gage didn't know what to think and he shot an accusing glance at Boomer. But before Gage could voice a question, out of the kitchen came Schiller, eyeing Gage like he'd been tagged on purpose. Schiller strolled over, showing every bit that this was his plan, and he was playing dirty.

"What's this all about?" Gage asked defensively.

"Relax kid." He placed an arm about Gage's wide shoulders and ushered him in, then pointed at the large tv that had been pushed in as far as it would fit in the living room blocking whatever tv actually resided in the home. Wires snaked up the side and into the computer that sat on top. On the screen a low-resolution image of a weightlifting meet-up was playing, pod casted in. Subtitles at the bottom of the screen gave out the stats of who topped in the last category as well as announced the Women's Super-Heavyweight coming up next. "You didn't think I would let you just walk out on us without a fight, did you?"

"You could have just said something."

"Something tells me you don't put a whole lot of value on words, and I am a damn good judge of character." Schiller smirked at him, then clinked Gage's beer bottle with his own before turning to give Boomer a handshake then went to sit down in one of the chairs.

"Oh, come, come, come." Lenora waved Gage and Boomer to move in further and join her. Lenora sat down smack in the middle on the sofa and Boomer took a spot next to her, but Gage chose to stand, just trying to take it all in. Two more people spilled out from the kitchen at the back of the house. Both carrying snack trays and bowls of chips. The food was set out on the coffee table then both, he and she, squished in next to Schiller. The woman had long since given her skin over to a tattoo artist and was pretty much covered in them, though now the colors had faded with years of sun exposure. Her blonde hair had one of those salon curlers styles so it kept neat and tight against her scalp and gelled for perfection. It was she who parked her round, plump butt in Schiller's lap, while the guy who'd accompanied her, took to one of the arms of the chair. His long silver streaked, ashen brown hair flowed well past his shoulders and down his arms with wavy telltale signs that said it'd been braided earlier. He was much thinner than the woman and the matching goatee added to his character as he leaned in to rest against Schiller. *Roberta and Charlie.*

There were about four or five others in the room, and they all tightened in as the announcer's voice came over the television that the next division was about to start.

"I wasn't aware this was being televised," Gage spoke out rather surprised watching the screen as both coaches, judges, and assistants milled over the stage in preparation.

"It's not. But they do have it on a podcast," Roberta spoke up. "So I just have the internet sourcing into the tv so everyone can watch.

"Oh sorry, where are my manners?" Schiller spoke up, wiping a dribble of his beer from his lips with the back of his hand as he shifted so he could look around Charlie to see Gage. "Gage, this here is my half, Roberta." He pointed a thumb to the man sitting next to him, "And this here is my other half," his hand rubbing her arm with a gentle caress, "Charlie." He pulled her to lean back some more so he could see better then began pointing at everyone around the room. "That's Willy, and that there's Ramon, and Clayton, Annette, Juanna. And of course, Lenora."

"Shh, shh, they're starting." Lenora waved her hand to quiet everyone.

The room varied in interest as each student on the podcast went up taking their turn at their lift. Each lifter was given three lifts each. Their score rated on the best out of three. All the girls in the Super Heavyweight were of similar size and build as Skye. One of the few sports where bigger was better.

Gage watched each intently, watching their form, the weight load, the approach, he knew just by watching and looking for the nuances if they were a contender to reckon with or just a number in line to have to wait on. A few crushed, others made clean lock outs. Luckily no injuries this round. But then several had played it safe. But that only meant they weren't going for the Olympics or YWC; or they already had enough points in the bag to ride this one out.

Next up was Skye, stepping up from backstage on top of the platform. She wore the full weightlifting compression suit uniform as standard for her sport. A thick padded leather belt wrapped low just under her midriff. Wrist supports on both arms and her knees were wrapped for further support. All items Gage hadn't allowed her to rely on while training; she needed to train without all the aids. However, they were still an important part of the sport. So having them on for the meet was not going to hurt her.

She was standing off to the sidelines, a man hunched down, talking to her as she shook her arms and legs, shaking off the nervous tensions, and getting the blood flowing as she waited for her cue.

*"Last up in tonight's Super Heavyweight: Skye Jackson for the Clean & Jerk,"* the commentator announced while her name and school appeared on the bottom of the screen.

"That's my baby!!" Lenora shouted out, jumping to her feet to do a jiggly dance, which for the large woman was a whole lotta jiggle.

On the television screen, Skye stepped up to the weight bar already set in place for her, two men to each side on standby to spot her. She lifted her arms up and punched at the air above her head, rolled her neck around then lowered down into her squat.

"Ooo, what's that stuff on her face?" Lenora called out.

Gage grinned as Boomer twisted to look up at him, "It's called a moko. The Samoans and New Zealand people wear them to show their strength and braveness." He answered about the black scribbling tribal design that'd been drawn on Skye's chin.

"That's the mojo you gave her?" Boomer asked.

Gage nodded. "It's probably not accurate with whatever the actual design is supposed to mean, but I wanted to give her something special, and that's all I could think of at the moment."

Lenora turned and raised an eyebrow at him, "You didn't take my baby to get a tattoo, did you?"

"No, ma'am, it's just a grease pen. It'll wash off but won't sweat off while she's competing."

"Quiet, all you!" Schiller barked and everyone watched as Skye pulled off her first lift set.

Her first *Clean* lift went right up to her chest, her feet adjusting, toes out then her legs drove up to begin the second part of the lift with the *Jerk*. Her arms following through, snapping the weights overhead into the lockout. The count registered and she let the bar drop before her, sending an echo of a crash through the gymnasium. Skye stepped back to shake it off and prepared for the second. It was a good lift, showing no press-out or back stepping, but the weight wasn't where she needed to impress anyone. She was still way inside the safe zone.

A tender nodded and Skye stepped up and took position, her fingers hovering over the bar, but she hesitated and suddenly stepped back.

"Oh, come on, baby, don't get scared now," Lenora called out to her daughter through the television set.

Skye was shown walking over to someone side stage and next the tenders were coming up and adding another plate to each side.

"That's it, Skye. Don't quit." Gage whispered.

The room grew tense as they watched Skye take position again. A moment of pause then with a shout the bar snapped up to her chest, her body sitting deep in the dip, then another cry and the heavy bar moved up. Her elbow dropped and Skye had to push for the lockout. It was good, but the commentator called the press out.

It wasn't a bad thing to anyone but, an Olympian scout. If the snap wasn't clean and the lifter had to press to reach the lockout, it would be a disqualification in an Olympic game.

"Press out? Is that bad?" someone in the room asked.

"Depends on who's watching tonight." This time it was Schiller who answered.

Skye stepped up for her third. A deeper concentration skittered across her face, she puffed out several deep breaths then rolled her lips in, holding the last breath, and started the lift. She moved faster this time, sending the snap up and into the lockout in a clean Jerk.

"You Go, Baby! Momma is so proud of you!!!!!!!" Lenora cheered with all the radiance a mother could have for a child.

There was no pause as the lifters were cycled back around for the next lift. The Snatch. Most of the girls did well, with only one crushing on all three of her lifts. The girl from one of the Penn state schools had been the one pushing the limits all night. *All or nothing.* She went in with all but hadn't been able to make the lockout.

The stakes were high and now it came down to the final lift set for Skye, and she had to go all or nothing.

Gage counted the plates— she was on the border. Enough to look good, but not to wow them.

She took her spot, hands taking the bar. She stared out in front of her, puffed out then sucked in a deep breath and— *"HUH!"* Skye cried out, the bar snapped into the lockout, feet shifted and then up! Making a clean snatch before letting it drop.

"YESH!!" several in the room shouted. All but Gage, Boomer, and Schiller. It was good, but not enough.

Skye's second lift was almost a near copy of the first, but still not enough to put her above the others. To a scout the girl who crushed was a better investment. The all or nothing gamble.

Gage shook his head. Even if Skye made a good clean Snatch on the third lift it wouldn't help her. And he watched helpless as she stepped up to the bar waiting for her. *Find it in you. You can do this and don't let anyone tell you different. Just don't quit.* The very words he'd kept telling her over and over again now resounded inside his own thoughts, wishing they'd do the same to her. *No one won from standing in the safe zone.* Then as if she had heard him, she walked off, right back over to one of the men on the side stage. And like before, the tenders stepped up and added another plate. But Skye didn't approach, she was still talking to him. Her coach came running up and stepped into the discussion. Whatever was going on, it didn't meet his approval. The discussion turned heated, but Skye kept steadfast to what she was asking for and before long the tenders were given instructions to add yet another plate to each end of her bar.

Gage was practically leaning over Boomer to count the plates before the sublet at the bottom of the tv screen confirmed it. 155kilograms.

"Shit! What are you doing, Skye?" Schiller muttered to the television.

Gage felt the charge in his body heating up as he watched, projecting all his energy and faith to Skye, hoping that somehow, she would feel it.  She was going for it, putting all her chips in. *All or nothing. Don't Quit!*

On the tv screen the camera showed Skye finally stepping up to the bar. Two men standing to each side, a third just behind them just in case. She swept her arms out, then in front to crisscross and back out to thwart the building tension. She rolled her shoulder then her neck, getting loosened up, then set her feet apart, and lowered down until she sat between her knees. Ass down— shoulders directly inline over her knees— her focus zeroed in on some invisible spot in front of her.

"Do a good job. Do a good job." Someone in the room was praying while another whispered the chant.

Gage wasn't any different as he locked onto every flicking muscle on Skye's body talking to him. *She was going to do this.*

*You keep going! Don't quit! Don't quit, Skye!*

Deep concentration intensified on her face. Fingers curled around the bar— gripped— adjusted— then gripped again. She puffed two or three times, sucked in a huge breath, held it, and then in a sudden explosion of energy, Skye cried out. Her body propelled up, snatching the bar straight up for the sky and in that same millisecond, her body dropped back down under the bar, setting her arms into the lockout. The weights held in a tight polar alignment over her shoulders and then in a second-winded burst, she went up with a war cry.

"YES!!! SHE DID IT! HA HA, SHE DID IT!" The living room filled with a mosh pit of cheers, while on the television screen, Skye stood triumphantly on the stage where several tenders and assistants gathered around her to congratulate her. Skye hadn't just done well for the meet; she had just beaten last year's Youth World Champion Gold Medalist's record. While someone within the YWC was likely to beat the record sometime soon, for a lifter still within the high school regionals, it was a triumph that wouldn't be taken lightly.

Gage leaned back against the wall letting out a happy sigh of relief and wiped the tear from the corner or his eyes, unable to shake the warm feeling he felt inside. A hand caught him, and he looked to see Boomer reaching out to him.

"You did that for her."

Gage only nodded softly. *No.* She *had done it.*

Schiller was right there next, taking Gage in a rough arm-n-arm shake then yanked him in for a bear hug. "You did a great job with her. Great job." And when Schiller pulled away, Gage could see the man was just as proud of him as he was of Skye Jackson.

With the event over, everyone fell into chatter.

Gage wandered into the kitchen to check out the rest of the food put out for grabs. His nose leading him to a fresh dish of pumpkin spice bread pudding covered with an oozing glaze that gave off the tangy aroma of oranges. "Mmmm—" he groaned with a happy-happy grin and volunteered to take it off Lenora's hands.

"You better stay in here and eat that if you aren't planning on sharing." She cocked her eyebrow at him, trying to hide her happy grin, then picked up one of the other casserole dishes and carried it out.

*"Hey, what happened to the bread pudding?"*

Gage overhead someone ask just as he tore off a gooey piece with his fingers and stuffed it into his mouth. *Ohhh, man it was good, he groaned to himself.*

*"I don't know what you're talking about."*

He heard Lenora's sarcastic reply sing out.

*"You're going to eat this instead and you're gonna like it."*

Gage could only chuckle and pushed more of the confiscated dessert between his lips. The warm pumpkin pie flavored goodness melting on his tongue and just the right amount of tangy zap from the citrus glaze was just out of this world.

"Ah huh should have known." Schiller was suddenly beside him barking and grabbing up a plate then a large spoon and served up a good helping of the bread pudding onto the plate.

"That's enough to feed three men your size." Gage scowled at his boss.

"I have to share with Boomer." He glared at Gage then went back out to the living room. Gage glanced down. Hardly what he would call a man size serving left, but quickly broke it up into bit size pieces. Just as he was about to pop one of those bites into his mouth, a large hairy arm reached over his shoulder and snatched it out of his hands then vanished. He twisted about just as the bear moaned exaggeratedly, chewing the morsel down.

"There are penalties for stealing anything pumpkin from me," Gage warned.

Boomer looked at him then to the pieces still in the dish with a playful expression like the temptation to try it was too much and, sure as shit, the man tried to sneak that big arm under Gage's nose to snatch another. Gage reached out catching him by the wrist before Boomer could escape with the stolen morsel. They locked eyes, Boomer tried to pull away. Gage put a bit of strength into his hold on Boomer, then slowly, in a silent match of strength, Gage began to lift Boomer's hand and the bite of bread pudding towards his own mouth. His arm shook with the tension as Boomer's own strength engaged to resist. Gage grinned, flexed his arm and curled his wrist in just enough that cost Boomer some of his own strength and the prize was suddenly in Gage's mouth as he closed his lips around *it*— and Boomer's fingers.

Boomer just stared at his own hand.

"Mmmm." Gage hummed, pushing his tongue around Boomer's fingertips before letting him pull away. He reached for the last bite in the pan and held it up for Boomer, who slowly started to reach for it. Gage pulled it away fast. "Ah, ah." Gage corrected Boomer and motioned with his head and a glance directed right at Boomer's mouth. "With your lips." then held the morsel back up and waited.

Boyishly shy blue eyes looked down him then at the offering and Gage could have sworn he saw the man's cheeks turn red.

Boomer sucked in a deep breath tucked his chin then turned and walked out.

Gage just stood there staring at the empty spot. Surprised it hadn't worked as he'd hoped. *Damn. Food always works.* He popped the last bite into his mouth and chewed for thought. It was probably for the best, Gage had every intention of pulling Boomer down for a kiss once he took the bait.

The night was hardly finished, everyone eventually milled to the back porch where more food, beer, and wine coolers waited for everyone. Music was pumped out stereo speakers, drug out the sliding glass doors, with some fun Jimmy Buffet party music.

Schiller and his two halves had already left as had Boomer, but Gage hadn't been given any sort of early escape options. Skye's mother just wouldn't have it.

He sat relaxing back in a tropical colored Adirondack chair. Lenora in another right next to him, as they drank and watched everyone else dance and just have a good time.

"So where is Skye's father? Does he know she competes?"

Lenore's smile didn't even falter like some women would as the low point of their story was revealed. She looked out over her friends as if to search the night sky for the man. "He's in Hawaii, but he doesn't even know she exists."

"That bad?"

"Oh no. That man was a moment in my life I will never forget." She smiled at him then reached into the ice bucket for a fresh wine cooler, then sat back and told her story. "Me and my home girl had been saving for two years. Determined to have a tropical vacay of a lifetime. After saving every penny we had, we booked one of those eight-night package deals with a travel agent to beautiful Hawaii." She sang out, "But just up before we were to go, Pamela fell sick." Lenora's smile drooped a bit and she glanced at him, trying as she could to keep from losing it all together then nodded, "She wouldn't let me not go. So, I did. My second night there I met this beautiful man at one of those luau parties. Oh, that man knew how to tear up the sheets and make a woman feel like a goddess." She laughed and her eyes glazed over as she stared out recalling her trip. "I'd never had a man make me feel so beautiful and sexy in all my life. Never felt it again, neither. It was the best seven days of my life." She laughed, "And wouldn't you know it, seven weeks later I was paying homage to the fertility gods in my bathroom every morning. I couldn't think of a more beautiful memento than that baby." She fell quiet a moment, half watching her family and friends still dancing around acting too silly with the music and half just letting her thoughts wander away.

"She gets her beautiful face from you, but her eyes—did she get those from the father?"

"Nope, his eyes were as dark and black as mine. When she was born and we'd seen her blue eyes, I knew then Angels had planned it all along. I've never regretted that holiday trip one bit. I met a very special man over there. I think that same angel must still be with me because now I have met two special men in my life." She leaned over and clinked her bottle to Gage's. "Thank you," she whispered then stretched over some more to plant a kiss on his cheek.

# 9

Gage's two-week notice had done gone and went. Now, instead of leaving Gage had found himself getting socked in the eye by one of the new guys coming in thinking he could upset the mojo that Gage and Boomer protected so possessively.

Gage sat on one of the benches while Boomer was playing doctor to his split brow.

"Didn't Schiller tell you; I keep the peace?"

"Yeah, yeah. I just thought the guy would see I was saving his ass from getting his pounded."

"You're not doing anyone no favors from protecting them from a whooping they earned."

Gage almost laughed because it sounded like something his mom used to say.

Boomer was about finished and pressed a couple of butterfly stitches across the split to hold it closed, making Gage wince a bit.

"You'll live," Boomer noted.

"Sure, but I'd heal better if you kissed it to make it better."

Boomer dropped his hand and just looked at him like he'd said something offensive.

"Boomer, I'm gay. Just like you. It's nothing to be afraid of."

Whatever the hell was going on in that head of Boomer's, Gage couldn't track for nothing. But he figured it meant Boomer wasn't interested.

"You'll live," Boomer said again, then gathered up the first aid kit and disappeared into his office. Leaving Gage to feel like shit for even suggesting it.

Then suddenly Boomer's office door swung back open, and he poked his head out. "You going to Schiller's party?"

"I haven't been invited."

"You can go with me then."

"Oh yeah?" Gage looked at him not sure how comical this should have been, "Will I get a kiss then?" He grinned hoping to lighten those loafers on the man a bit.

Boomer fudged up his face in a way that made the bear's boyish eyes lose their grumpy scowl and all the more adorable. His expression seemed to melt into an oblivion of unknowing, then, before Gage might catch any sign or telling redness, Boomer vanished once more behind the door without giving an answer.

Saturday afternoon at the Highlander Game festival was a good place to be and Gage couldn't think of a better place for Schiller and his two partners to celebrate their anniversary. Where everyone could just have some fun. The bonus was getting to see the twins: Mitch and Mike, plus a few others from the gym, compete. *ManCandy in kilts. Hell yes*. Only the perks didn't end there, the kegs of lager and pit roasted food were bottomless— but all that was nothing, because Gage had Boomer with him.

It was hard to put into perspective, when here he was, a grown man, yet sitting here like some twelve-year-old virgin kid finding it super difficult to think of something to say to his crush without it coming out sounding completely ridiculous. It was even worse when his boss could see it and was having a few ball-cracking jokes over it. At one point, Gage just gave up with trying to be smooth and grabbed Boomer's hand in his to hold it.

When Schiller snickered at him, Gage thought for sure he was going to go over and pummel the man. But to Schiller's saving, Charlie, and Roberta both did it for him.

The hand holding had turned out to be a good move and they were soon arm and arm if not exactly talking about anything beyond what everyone else was talking about. They were both playing it cool, holding each other as if not. *It was totally ridiculous, but funny.* As the night came and the festival's bonfires were lit, Boomer was doing more leaning than holding.

The group had wandered off, leaving Gage and Boomer some space.

"You remember when you asked me to kiss you?"

"I remember."

"Do you still—"

Gage didn't even let him finish before closing the gap between them.

Boomer seemed uncertain at first but was soon melting against Gage's lips. Large arms came up around Gage, holding and leaning all at once, while Gage held on wanting to sweep the man off his feet in just their first kiss. The embrace was laced with lager and fire cooked ham. Neither of which bothered him at all. He'd rather kiss a well-lived man than one who'd doused his breath with mints.

Gage felt himself being pulled down and he twisted so Boomer landed on the top of the picnic table where they sat. Only it was then when Gage felt Boomer's involvement in the make-out slough away. The kiss died between them, and Gage leaned up a bit to see what had changed. *Damned if he didn't feel the cock-blocking curse again.*

He let out a heavy sigh, trying his best not to laugh as he sat back up, planting his elbows to his knees, and surrendered his chin to his clasped hands. He just sat there, listening as the sounds of a bear, who apparently couldn't hold his lager, snoring away in hibernation— sawing logs behind him.

# 10

Today, like every Monday before this one, Gage stood just behind Jamal watching his form as he did his reps of quadricep and glute squats along with the extra 50lbs they'd just added to the man's shoulder bar. "Bring your stance out a little further," Gage instructed, still keeping one hand up to follow where the bar went just in case, he needed to take the weight, while the young man adjusted his feet before going down again.

Jamal was one of his more dedicated athletes. Young, with dreams of football stardom in mind, so when he wasn't out on the field practicing, he was in here for strength training. And from what some of the other guys had told Gage, while Jamal only played varsity at a lesser-known state college, he had managed to catch the attention of a few bigger university scouts and next year held some promises for him.

Schiller came out of his office, oblivious to the world around him, but stopped dead in his tracks when the iconic Neanderthal was not in his rightful spot. Schiller twisted, fist on his hips and looked around. A scowl crept over his brow when he wasn't spotting who he wanted. "Anybody know where Boomer is?" he called out to no one in particular.

Gage, along with half a dozen other guys, looked up and only shrugged, but no one gave an answer.

"Well, where the fuck is he?" Again no one answered and after a few seconds all the blank stares went back to their own private thoughts and work out; all except Gage.

Even after Schiller grabbed something from behind the counter and disappeared back into his office, Gage's attention returned to the unnatural empty spot behind the register. What should have been there was a massive Bear standing all of 6'8" tall and roughly 3' wide. One he'd just recently kissed.

Six months Gage had been here now and not once had Boomer ever missed a day of work. And while everyone else may not have given it much thought, he did.

Gage glanced up at the wall clock. It was already fucking quarter past three. Not even the most common excuses would make Boomer more than two hours late. Not that Gage had ever known Boomer to use a single one of them. Boomer wasn't exactly an on-the-minute kind of guy, but he had the whole lunch hour to arrive. As long as he was in by one, to which he always was.

Jamal stopped his reps and Gage kicked into autopilot to help in returning the bar back to the rack. "Go ahead and put the plates back. We're going to work with the medicine ball the rest of the day." His attention went back to the register then to the front door as if expecting to see Boomer walk in any minute now. Expecting Boomer'd most likely be pissed off about someone or something for making him late.

Maybe someone parking in the handicapped space now that the gym had a new member that needed it. Elliot had joined just a week ago, wanting to run and compete track. Near every trainer in the area had sent him packing. Apparently, someone told Elliot that Gage was capable of knocking that chip off his shoulder, something that nobody else was willing to do to a guy in a wheelchair. To Gage, Elliot was just another man and if he was gonna be a dick then he deserved to get punched. It didn't quite come to that, but Gage had earned the man's respect and Elliot found the coach that wasn't going to coddle him or let him off easy just because he was missing both his legs from the knees down.

But as it were, Boomer never walked through the door. And Gage's gut felt something was wrong. He knew the feeling because he'd felt it once before.

Jamal came back, medicine ball in hand, and thrust forward at Gage who snapped it back, "Ain't fucking happening, light weight. Put the kiddy ball back and go get the right one." Gage tossed the under weighted ball back to the kid.

Jamal chuckled, "Just keeping ya on yo' toes, coach."

"More like testing to see if I'll let you slide out easy for once."

"Hey man, I got a date tonight. Girl so fine I gotta save some strength for her." Jamal's mouth quirked up in a half shit-eating grin.

"What's more important? Having a marathon fuck session tonight or goin' pro next year?"

"*Mahhhn*— ya'll honky boys just don't seem to get the importance of a black man's dick." Jamal tossed his hands down and went back to the shelf along the wall and grabbed the next ball two sizes up and tossed it from where he was standing.

Gage caught it, feeling the intense weight and the challenge that sent it to him. He returned it with equal gusto and a burst of laughter, "You think my pumpkin spice dick doesn't like to get wet?"

Jamal went back to his spot on the mat, shifting the medicine ball to one hand and hurled it to Gage on the next pass. "I don't know, man. Some of the guys be sayin' you be likin' other guys. I mean, how wet can it get?"

Gage laughed again, exchanged hands on the ball and tossed it back in-like-form as Jamal had, "I assure you, when I cum in it, it's extremely wet."

Jamal expressed his unwillingness to imagine it with an exaggerated shiver and missed the toss, "Feel free *not* to get too personal and share yo' sex life with me." He waved Gage off then went to retrieve the ball and started the back and forth toss again. "Sorry, no disrespect dude, but I prefer pussy."

"None taken, but are you seriously going to tell me you never fucked your girlfriend's ass?"

Jamal caught the ball and sent it back. "One: she ain't my girlfriend. Two: yes, I have fucked an ass before, and it's nice. I admit."

Gage caught the ball and held onto it, looking Jamal straight up. "It's nice all the time."

Jamal quirked up an eyebrow at him. "Oh, alright. I see where this is at, you just got a thing for balls."

They both laughed as Gage nodded in agreement, and then waved Jamal over taking a new position with their backs to each other. Gage twisted and passed the weighted ball to Jamal now behind him who took it, twisted the other way and passed it back around. They kept this up adding in variations of movement, overhead, over the shoulder around the side between the legs. But Gage's eyes went to the mirrored wall and to the reflection of the counter and the man who wasn't there. *Why was it suddenly that when the man wasn't here that Gage couldn't get him off his mind?*

# 11

The next day Boomer was in like clockwork, like nothing out of the ordinary had happened. Although something clearly had. He was quieter than usual, and there was pain lurking in his blue eyes. Nonetheless, no one asked, and he never offered any explanation. But what he did do took them all by surprise. After clocking in and going through the routine of reading over the notes from the morning opener, followed with a count in the register, Boomer came out of the supply room with a wall hanger and hammer.

He tore all the flyers and the one fitness poster down from the wall next to his register, brushed the wood paneling off with a rag— eye balled where to set the wall hanger— a couple of taps on the nail and then, as if he was unwrapping the Mona Lisa, he gently produced an 8x10 framed picture from a bag and hung it up on the wall.

Gage had tried to talk to him, but Boomer wouldn't have it, waving him back to take trainees as per his job, while Boomer remained behind the counter guarding the picture frame he'd so carefully hung.

Gage didn't dare get curious until after Boomer had gone home for the day. Something just told him not to even tempt fate. At 7:00pm on the dot, Boomer locked up the register, turned the front outside lights off and left, leaving everyone else to clean up without even a *good night, fellas*.

Gage dropped everything and went up to see what Boomer had guarded over all day. What he found sent him into all kinds of confusion over the complex and quiet man.

In the photo, Gage was staring at the over-sized bear-cub sitting with a warm and happy boyish grin hidden behind a mountain of facial hair. Behind him, snuggling with arms draped over his shoulders in a tight hug stood a chunky blonde-haired girl only half his size with the same grin. Only the rounded-out chin and shape of her matching blue eyes revealed she had Down syndrome. *It was Abigail.* The one who always played with the guys about the super suit.

Gage just stared at it, summoning up some vague memory of one of her visits to the gym a few months back. She was standing alongside Boomer up at the front door about to leave. Gage recalled how she reached up patting at him with both hands, like a little kid would, to get your attention, and her prodding worked, as Boomer hunkered down low enough to let those chubby little arms wrap around his neck to hug him, then she planted a big kiss on his cheek before leaving.

It hadn't been the first time he'd seen Boomer oblige her affection. Gage had simply thought Abi had a crush on Boomer and thought nothing of it. Just like Joshua who always came up and gave Gage a hug. But there was some form of pride— a deeper connection glowing in Abi's face as she posed with Boomer in the photo.

"Whatever you do, don't ever let Boomer catch you staring at that photo." Schiller's voice came up behind him.

Gage spun around, unable to mask the surprised expression he felt or the shock that his boss was still here, adding to the collection of strange behaviors today. "Who is she?"

Schiller reached past Gage and pulled the frame from the wall. He looked at it for a long moment, even his thumb graced over the face of the girl with some fondness. "Boomer's mom."

All the air left Gage just then as if Schiller had just slapped him on the chest. Gage could have made a thousand guesses and *mom* would not have been one of them. "His mom? Seriously?"

Schiller bobbed his head silently then set the frame back to its hook. "Abigail Thurston, daughter to a prominent do-gooder, New England family. She was raped when she was only fourteen. Boomer was the product of that vile act." Schiller leaned over the counter, planting his elbow and relaxed his weight on it with a thoughtful look about him as his eyes dropped to the floor and recanted the mile markers of Boomer's life. "Abi's well-to-do folks didn't believe in abortions, but they didn't want her to keep it either. And since she was a minor, what Abi wanted didn't matter. They didn't even see to it the baby got a proper home. Just took it to the parish and left it there. Father Mohan down at the Irish Presbyterian church knew though, and he kept track of the boy. He'd gotten adopted, his new family gave him the name Todd, but by the time Boomer was three he landed back at an orphanage. From there, he went from foster home to foster home. Boomer's size was a large bearing on his being shuffled about. I suppose his introvert quietness was another. When he was fifteen, he'd gotten caught having sex with another boy his age, and he was tossed from yet another foster home. That's when he showed up back here, looking for his mother— and answers I suppose." Schiller took in a deep breath, holding it a second before letting it out. "Guess he wasn't expecting to find a mother with Down syndrome neither. If he felt anguish about being abandoned when he came back, the answer he got was enough for him to make an about face in the way he looked at things after. Abi's folks, however, were not pleased with him showing up at their doorstep. Abi, on the other hand, couldn't have been happier and all her years of depression vanished with the very first hug from her lost son."

"Known him long, I take it?"

"Yep, been knowing Boomer a long time." Schiller rubbed across his lips, then pushed off the counter.

He squatted down to grab a box from under the counter, tossing it up top, and started unloading the bottles of vitamins and enhancers to restock the display case behind them while he continued on with Boomer's story. "I'm not sure how it all got started, but at some point, Abigail got one of those emancipation orders against her parents, then got set up in an assisted living apartment and Boomer moved in with her. Boomer got back in school part time and started working down on Market Street, loading and unloading trucks. He took care of Abi, and she became the most loving mother a wounded lost boy could ever ask for. Together, they found the happiness they'd both been searching for and needing. Things were right for them."

"So, what's changed?"

Schiller returned the box to its hiding spot, closed up the glass case, and locked it. He turned back looking at Gage, his face sullen, "He promised he'd never leave her to an institution, and he's kept his promise." Schiller stilled, took another deep breath and sighed, "Lock up, will ya?"

"For a boss man you seem to know things about him that an average man, not even a boss, should know." Gage spoke out that he wasn't buying the casual overseer story. Boomer had been so recluse about his personal life that it would take more than just anyone to know that much about the man. "Who are you to him?"

Schiller sucked in a deep breath, then scratched over the silver chest hairs, peeking out over the top of his cut-up t-shirt. "Boomer is my nephew. My brother was the one who'd raped Abigail. I've been trying to make some rights for that boy ever since he was born." He turned and without another word left for the night, leaving Gage in the dim lighting of the gym, alone with his thoughts and a picture of a woman with a young mind, holding the world's biggest Teddy Bear.

Gage realized, that as a society, people go through life often never even realizing who a person is though they'd been standing there all along. Like the stories you hear about the man next-door— been there for twenty years. All of a sudden, it's in the news; the dude's gone bonkers and the neighbors are all saying: *He always seemed like an okay guy.*

Gage kept staring at the photograph of Boomer and his mother. Right now, Gage was having just such a moment about the man he worked with. He'd been working with Boomer for six months and just now realized he hadn't known the first damn thing about him. But one thing was for sure, a man with a mother like Abigail Thurston had to have a soft spot and Gage was now determined to get to know that side of the oddly, quiet giant.

# 12

Boomer staying at the gym late today was about as strange as him not showing up for work at all just four days ago. Aside from the odd change in behavior, Boomer was becoming a considerably deeper distraction for Gage. As in, he had a newfound understanding, which was more than just a liking to looking at him.

The *looking* part had not been unsatisfactory. After all, what wasn't there to like?  If you had an eye for Bears, Boomer could fill that need and then some. Just mapping out the man's oversized body would take some time to explore— all six feet and eight inches of him. Not to mention, the chore it would likely take to get past all the over-protective guardian, moody, aggressive, reclusive introvert man just to get to the warm boyish smile that was in the photograph. *Grrr* — what Gage would do if he could just get his hands on the burly behemoth! Gage felt he'd either: snuggle the fuck out of him, or just snuggle up with his own face planted in that chest of fur for hours— *then* fuck him. *There was a considerable difference.*

Gage sat on one of the work-out benches, wiping down the plates with a cleaning rag soaked with disinfectant, but his eyes were across the way to Boomer. That soft carpet of brown fur always managed to call out to him from under whatever shirt Boomer happened to be wearing that day. Today was an orange t-shirt day, which, ironically, was Gage's favorite color. Just chalk up one more thing that continued to lure his eyes back over to Boomer when he should be paying attention to what he was doing so he could get his clean up finished and call it a night.

But back to the chest fur— it matched the heavy dust on Boomer's arms. Even the beard looked soft, and it was kept groomed rather nicely with an Irish smooth touch. All that hair and Gage could still make out the boyish face hidden underneath. A feature not even his age could cover over, his eyes especially. Nevertheless, over the past few days something inside Boomer was wounded and needed to be touched, but Gage had yet to see anyone try, and he wasn't sure about making the attempt himself. Approaching Boomer was a challenge all by itself. Just today, someone said something that set him off. And in one fell swoop, Boomer knocked the guy's lights out. Just one punch was all it took, and the dude was down for the count.

Gage hadn't planned on staying at the gym much longer, but if Boomer was, he'd stick around just to see if any connection might come about. While Boomer made frequent trips from the office to the fridge in the break room to retrieve yet another pint of beer, Gage decided to order up a pizza. Leaving the money on the counter for Boomer to find when the delivery arrived. Maybe his developed taste for bizarre pizza cravings would strike up a conversation between them.

Seeing he had a few minutes before the pizza arrived, he went over to one of the bench presses to knock out a few reps and pass the time.

He was barely breaking a sweat when he heard Boomer go to the door to unlock it. A quick exchange and then it was locked back up.  "Mind if I grab a slice?" Boomer called out from the front.

"Help yourself—" Gage answered, racking the weight bar and curled out from under it to sit up, taking his towel and wiping his arms down, "but I don't think your gonna like the toppings." He twisted, tossing the towel on his gym bag so he wouldn't forget it, only to turn back with an unexpected surprise when he was being hoisted off the bench by an angry huffing Boomer, who then carried Gage across the room and slammed him up against the wall.

"What the fuck are you trying to pull here?" Boomer leaned his weight against Gage, pinning him.

When the initial, *what the fuck,* wore off, Gage couldn't help but think if it weren't for Boomer being pissed off about something, his dick would be getting hard right about now. Just that one spoiler, knowing when Boomer gets pissed, things or people don't usually come out grinning with their teeth intact. However, when Boomer shifted so one leg pressed between Gage's thighs, that's when Gage felt the rise of blood flow and was reminded his dick really didn't give a shit if Boomer was about to pound his face in. Because pissed or not, getting slammed against the wall by this bear was hot as fuck.

Still, he'd like to know what he was about to get battered for, first. He wrapped his fingers around Boomer's wrists and with some considerable effort pried the man off of him. His dick wasn't all that thrilled about it either. "What's just gotten into you, Boomer?" Gage asked, tossing Boomer's hands aside.

"The pizza!" Boomer scoffed.

Gage shrugged with a bewildered shake of his head, "What about it? It's pizza. Albeit, it is weird, but I said you could have some if you wanted." That's when he found himself slammed right back against the wall again.

"Exactly. Weird— as in your playing games with me and I don't care for anyone to be trying to fuck with me!"

*Fucking with him? Over pizza toppings?* This didn't make any sense and Gage wasn't about to get pummeled for it. "Unless you're planning on nailing me to the wall for some hardcore sex, maybe you'll explain why my pizza has you so pissed off."

Boomer let go instantly and backed off. Some strange emotions tearing across the man's face— *a confession he wasn't ready for, perhaps*. His mouth twitched to the side a few times and the heat seemed to dispel along with it, and he turned to go back to the counter where the pizza waited for them. "How is it you like pineapple, ham, artichokes, and banana peppers on pizza?"

*Okay, so it was a fair question, perhaps a worth telling if it would earn Gage a* get-out-of-ER *free card.*

Gage walked up to join him, flipping the box open and pulled out the first slice and took a bite. Story or not he preferred his pizza while it was still hot. "Way back after I first moved here, I had gotten someone else's pizza by mistake with those toppings on it. But the delivery guy was long gone by the time I realized it." Gage took another bite and chewed with a thoughtful groan. "I was so damn hungry— I ate it anyways. I know it seems weird, but the shit's good. Just try it. If you don't like it, I will order you a pepperoni and mushroom." The fact that Gage liked it was still a mystery even to himself and wasn't something he always wanted to eat, but on occasion, he gave in to his strange craving for the weird combo.

Boomer huffed, "No fooling?" The sound he made was like a chuckle that got lost in the effort.

"Hand to god, straight up what happened." Gage raised his hand, palm open.

"That was my mom's pizza you got. We were stuck with the pepperoni and mushrooms." He grabbed a slice, but dropped it back down, and took off for the break room. He returned, hands loaded down with two more pints of beer, plus a couple of condiments in his hand.

The small spice bottle, in particular, caught Gage's attention and instantly held his hands out to defend the pizza, "No, no, no, no— what are you doing?"

Boomer brushed Gage's arms out of the way, and tried again, only to have Gage grab the jar along with the giant hand that held it. "No, no, no— we do not put nutmeg on the pizza!"

Boomer managed to divert Gage with little effort then doused the pizza until it was covered in the brown spice that oddly matched the color of the man's hair.

"You can't eat it without it, I'm telling you." The follow up was parmesan cheese, and then the seasoning on just Boomer's half.

"What is that?" Gage asked a little more curious since it *wasn't* added to his side of the pizza.

Boomer held it up for him to see the dried red flakes. "Hot pepper."

"Well, put it on my slices too, those help burn carbs."

Boomer almost managed to smile and sprinkled some of it on Gage's side of the pizza then watched as Gage picked up his first slice and inspected it. A sniff— a face wrinkle, and then finally took a bite.

Now Gage didn't have a clue what to expect, having his pizza dusted heavily with nutmeg. The idea just was impossible to grasp, then again, he was eating a pizza with pineapple, ham, artichokes, and banana peppers. So, what was one more oddity— but Boomer was right— the additive rang true as necessary, as if he'd come to some master-chef revelation upon discovering the final ingredient to a perfect freak-pizza. Just don't ask him to ever try to explain it. But it was damn good.

They ate in silence, groaning and chomping away on slice after slice, along with a side of cheese-stuffed bread sticks dipped in artery-choking garlic butter then washed it down with cheap lager. Frankly it was the best unspoken 2nd date Gage had had in a long time.

Gage rubbed at his belly and decided he would let Boomer have the last slice. At Boomer's size, Gage was certain he could put away some groceries and then the oddest thing caught his attention. "Mind if I ask something?"

Boomer half grimaced, half shrugged, but gave the all-nodding go-ahead signal.

"What's with the damn poster?" Gage tossed a thumb over in a haphazard, directed point towards *The Incredibles* poster that still had its spot near the door.

Boomer glanced over his shoulder and like a toggle switch, a huge grin popped out from underneath the thick beard. He folded his arm slow on his chest and leaned one elbow down on the counter until it creaked then lightened his weight a bit. His expression went to some memory in the past, but Gage could see it was a good one. "My mom gave that to Schiller as a birthday present one time. She likes to come in and cheer for the guys when they practice. The poster is from one of her favorite movies. She'll always tell the guys; they should maybe all go down to the train tracks to work out to get really strong like Mr. Incredible." Boomer paused, he scratched lazily at his temple with a finger and then an almost sad chuckle came up while his eyes shot down to the floor. "They always call out to her— *Where's my supersuit?*"

Gage finally got it. The shouting game must have been a scene from the movie. He watched Boomer draw quiet; he figured a change in subject might be in order. "So, the parking spot out front that's reserved for her?"

Boomer bucked up a bit, but only just, those blue eyes glancing up for the first time at him, "I told her no matter what, I will always have a spot saved for her."

"The white van always uses it. Does she have a car too?" Gage acted surprised, if for no other reason than to just keep the air light.

Boomer chuckled, straightening up to his feet and grabbed the last slice of pizza, "No, but no matter what, she has a parking spot saved in case she ever did, or whenever she gets a ride. It didn't matter really. Just as long as she knows.

Gage felt a kind of laugh inside, the one that makes you feel okay and happy, but you don't really make a sound. It's just a feeling, he guessed. But as he watched Boomer shovel down the last slice, he realized that six months of watching this brooding man growl and pound a few heads together, that there was a much softer side to him. Kinda like one of those chocolate candies with the hard shell and soft, gooey, good stuff inside.

Boomer wiped his hands on a paper towel and tossed it into the box and closed it up with a motion of finality. "Go on, get out of here. I'll clean up." He grabbed the empty pizza box in one hand and managed three of the empty pints in the other and carried them over to the large, grey trash can at the door.

Gage had no intention of leaving just yet. Truth be known, Boomer wasn't exactly an open door to get all buddy-buddy with. However, right now, he was finally getting to know this big Bear and he wasn't ready to just call it a night with him. If at all possible, Gage was hoping to stretch out this window of opportunity, that maybe, he would have some success with Boomer; anything to get the man to notice him. Even if it took an all-out pass at him to get there.

"Actually, I'm thinking on taking a shower, wanna come?" *Pun intended.*

Boomer paused, and then leaned back against the door, stuffing his hands into his jeans like he was some permanent fixture there; a normal posture for him that added to the boyish air under all the hair. "Maybe, is your whole body covered in those freckles?"

Gage let out a chuckle, nodding with pride for his dots. He grabbed the counter, steadying himself while he toed off his shoes then stood there wriggling his freckled toes in a playful movement to invite Boomer's eyes to look all he wanted. He grinned up at Boomer, then grabbed his shorts and everything else with them, and bent over, pushing them down around his ankles. When he stood, he gave Boomer another half-smile, hoping to invite the man's eyes to see for himself, "I'll even let you play connect the dots." Because he was most definitely covered in the heavy drops of orange and brown freckles.

Gage hadn't really put much thought into what he was doing, more like he was letting his internal male, pig comraderies go into horny autopilot for what he wanted. *Typical male thought process there. No geniuses added for certain.* So when Boomer started moving and came at him, there was an element of, —*OH SHIT!*— sounding off inside Gage's head. Because Boomer, at his size, was capable of clearing a room in just two strides and was now standing with hardly a dozen inches between the two of them. And frankly, it was hard to dispel the recent sight of seeing the man send another to the floor in one unblockable punch. As much as Gage wanted to have a go with Boomer, the thought that he may have just offended him or that he might find himself bottoming to an angry Boomer wasn't very appealing right now; he just wasn't into getting his ass pummeled any more than he was to have his face crushed.

But, as Gage stood his ground and glanced up at him, all he saw was a gentle giant that didn't have the first idea of where to put his hands. Before long, after some minor hesitating, Boomer's hands decided to take his own shirt off. He grabbed the bottom of his orange t-shirt in both hands and peeled it up over his head. Gage cursed, using a few more expletives like —*Woof*— because *dammit* he was in fur-baby heaven just drooling over the world of soft brown that covered Boomer's chest and stomach, and Gage was certain it kept on going. *Okay, so maybe he would reconsider giving in to bottom if that's what it took*, because damn, he was craving to have all the fuzz rubbing against him. Front or back— didn't matter.

From the time when Gage was a kid and just as puberty started to cause havoc in him, he started to develop a sense of likes and dislikes. He created a fantasy in his head and as he grew, the fantasy shifted and changed and went through a whole slew of modifications. Maturing as he grew older until finally at some point the fantasy stopped, because he had developed that perfect image of what he would love his man to look like. Never mind all that horse shit about love was supposed to make him blind and love no matter what they look like, this was about that ideal— *things that he liked and caught his eye, as well as his dick's attention*, and it's that designer look that always managed to turn his head.

Gage was speechless he couldn't put one foot in front of the other to walk away, because standing right here in front of him was *that* finely tuned fantasy. Boomer was thick and beefy. That was a detail that just couldn't get overlooked. And when Gage reached out and dove his hands into Boomer's chest, he discovered it was the softest damn fur he'd ever encountered. But that wasn't all— it just kept on going down over a soft belly and then disappeared down into Boomer's jeans.

Before he could think better of it, Gage buried his face in Boomer's chest; rubbed his cheeks in all that goodness while reaching up behind Boomer's neck and pulled that scruffy head down for a kiss. He was met with timid lips, tainted with brew, but as Gage brushed his body against Boomer's, letting his other hand wander about, Boomer finally opened up and relaxed into him, letting Gage lead.

There was just one flaw in Gage's fantasy, and it pricked momentarily in the back of his mind, just minutes before his brainless head took over. He was relatively an 80% top, and he already knew full well what it was like being in a relationship with a man who was 100% a top. The present clash was a dark reminder just how unsuccessful and unfulfilling it had been. However, as Boomer helped Gage rid his body of his own shirt, logic wasn't drawing the cards right now, and the thought was soon dismissed as both Gage and Boomer headed towards the shower, doing away with the remainder of Boomer's clothes along the way.

There was an overtone of awkwardness between them as they both stepped under the steaming water, watching the other's pelt turn slick against their skin. Boomer seemed mesmerized just following the cascade of freckles until his eyes landed firmly on Gage's cock, thick, but still bumping lazily against his thigh. The real oddity was Gage wasn't sure who was in charge here, just like the time at the party, Boomer was anything but stereo typical of sexually aggressive. Boomer, for all his size and ability to beat the shit out of any man, was now a passive giant, not the aggressive fuck Gage had figured on. So, he found himself leading a bit just to keep the embers stoking and building between them. They seemed to take a considerably long time just feeling each other over— *and up*— yet at the same time, Gage was holding back, and he wasn't sure why.

Of course, discovering Boomer was well proportioned reminded him, again, he was not going to be fond of the receiving end if it came to that. But the monster sized dick was a hell of a lot of fun to play with right now. And the growl that rumbled deep inside Boomer's chest was just downright fucking awesome.

Boomer never stopped in his fascination to just watch their bodies sliding against each other. And his hands did much of the same, as if attempting to caress every freckle on Gage's body individually. The results had Gage's dick standing on end in no time.

"I love your freckles." Boomer mumbled like they were man poetry or something and Gage reciprocated by raking his fingers into Boomer's chest hair. And they both watched for the orange dots to show through the dark brown forest. It was rather fun actually. He then slid his hands around Boomer's back side scooping up both cheeks of his ass and enjoying some firm groping. Boomer moaned, his head falling back a bit, "Oh yes— that feels nice."

Gage took advantage of the invitation, pressing his fingers further until he was tracing a line into the crack of Boomer's ass to tease over the tight pucker, and he soon felt Boomer's considerably larger arm reaching around to do the same to Gage.

The heat kicked up between them as they teased each other's holes, their cocks caught between them, and Gage had to admit as scary at that massive cock was, it was the hottest fucking thing a man could ever wish to frot against. Monster cocks just found a new lustful purpose in his toy box ideas of things to do. It just didn't get any more accommodating than this did. At least, he didn't think so. But, when an equally large hand wrapped around the both of them and began to stroke them off in a slow, kindling pace— that was when Gage realized he might not make it very long in all this. Then again, he sure as hell wasn't going to complain, because it was most definitely the hottest frigging and frotting he could have imagined having with this man and they'd only just begun.

The walls of the shower echoed with their growling and groaning. Boomer's thick finger moved inside Gage's ass, straightening with a flick that managed to catch his glory spot a couple of times, which had Gage tearing away from the tangle of tongue, hissing with a heavy pant then dove back into their kiss for some more.

It was a strange oddity to be encapsulated by this man who was nearly double his mass, and he was no small man himself. But Boomer assuredly eclipsed him, yet so far, he had not enforced any level of control, just the shared pleasure that was being delivered rather than a struggle to cop his own nut.

While visions of being balls deep inside Boomer filled Gage's heady desires and fired off more burning hunger in him, the hand that still wielded their cocks was about to see him to the finish line. The drawing up of his sack as it tightened against his body and that sweet pinch of lightning in his ass was all too near. "Damn, I'm so close. Do you want to cum with me, Boomer?"

"Yes-ss." The answer was moaned into their kiss.

Gage shoved Boomer's hand aside, taking both shafts into his own palm and began to stroke them over with a more fervent pace. He reached further around Boomer's backside to get a second finger into Boomer's ass, sliding in with as much of a scissoring as he could manage within the dizzying spell that Boomer's more dominant reach was doing to his own hole.

Boomer's head dropped back, his body slammed into Gage and then went rigid as he bellowed out a tight growling curse.

Gage felt the hot jizz pulse out of the thick cock, spilling over his hand and became instantly mixed into the stroking then within seconds, Gage's own release followed.

He clenched up, then succumbed to the tell-tale rattling that went through him like a tidal wave of gravel, while Boomer's hands stroked over Gage's back and chest obviously loving the playground of shivering chills.

They basked silently in the afterglow, washing each other off, but soon the distance started to set in. They quietly got dressed, and went back out to the front counter, pausing to kiss, if for no other reason than to prevent the afterglow from getting completely lost in the silence between them. But that seemed to take a trip south when Boomer turned away, closing himself inside the office with little more than a request for Gage to lock up on the way out.

Gage was just about to step out when he heard Boomer's office door creek open, and he saw Boomer standing there with his head hanging out.

"Gage?"

"Yeah, Boomer."

"Thanks." His affect seemed sad and rather distant, and then he withdrew back inside his hiding spot.

Gage was left to ponder what this all really meant and more than a little grateful that tomorrow was Saturday, and they didn't have to work. At least they had the weekend to just accept that perhaps this had just been stress-release sex.

Gage locked the place up, trying his best not to get bitter. Not about Boomer or about the not quite all-the-way sex or that it wouldn't lead to anything other than just more fooling around. He was all for having an active sex life. But he found himself anguishing over a false fucking hope that there was more than this gay ginger deserved. Once more, for a futile moment of thought, he had managed to fool himself into feeling he could have something great, and he had somehow thought Boomer could be it.

He shook his head, letting out a heavy sigh, disregarding his thoughts and misguided emotions, then kicked his bike to start it up and pulled off to head home— *alone*.

# 13

What motivated him to come to the cemetery today was unclear, but here he was and resolved it was long overdue.

Gage noticed the one-man funeral taking place on the far end of the lawn as he made his way along the winding path towards the back. Something about the grief-stricken figure pulled on Gage's thoughts. A towering shadow standing there all alone, save for the priest, standing opposite of the man, reading out the prayers. The man looked so tall standing there by himself and yet, his slunk shoulders didn't hide just *how* broken he was.

Gage snapped his attention back to the direction he was going before he got caught staring and he headed down the winding path to the memory of his own loss.

It'd been a while since he'd come out here and it touched him with a bit of guilt, even though it'd been a little over seven years since Michael was killed while driving drunk.

When he reached the spot, Gage dropped down to his knees and set to the task of plucking a few scraggly weeds from the base of the headstone, dusted it off with his fingers then set the bag of fast food down in front of it. "Here. Extra cheese this time." He sat back on his heels, glancing around, seeing a few people here and there, walking or doing much the same as he was. Perhaps doing it better.

He twisted, looking back up the hill to the lone man up top. Even from here, Gage could feel the man wasn't just sad but lost, and again Gage felt some small amount of guilt, because he couldn't remember if he ever felt that much grief when they lowered Michael down into the ground.

He sucked in a deep breath and let a heavy sigh out as he turned back to the tombstone, even traced the engraved letters with a finger before dropping his hand down on his leg. He was sure he had, but Michael had never been everything he wanted. They had a good relationship, but far from the greatest, just always managing to make it by with each other. Sometimes they'd even argue about that, but it always came back to the beliefs that society had instilled in them. *That being gay didn't come with promises of love. That if you found someone who was at least willing to hang around then you needed to be happy with that and get over yourself.* And no matter how Gage tried to believe and hope for something better, there were still those times when doubt won. Because after all was said and done, here he was— alone. The epitaph *Don't Quit,* didn't work here.

The reality of he and Michael was they were as good of a match as two north ends of a magnet. Great friends, horrible fuck buddies. For starters, they were both tops. Gage didn't mind switching to take bottom every once in a while, but Michael was anything but an enjoyable bottom and would sometimes fight to the bitter end of the night, until neither of them wanted to even be in the same bed, let alone fuck or snuggle. At some point, Gage came to realize, years later, it wasn't really about who was top or bottom in the fucking, it was Gage needed a connection that Michael was never willing to be a part of. Gage liked to cuddle; he was an easy laid-back man who just liked touching. Even after a solid energy exhausting round of sex, Gage had often attempted to lure Michael into some post-coital spooning, but Michael would have nothing to do with it.

How they stayed together for four years, there was no telling, and once more Gage found himself coming full circle to that argument that gays don't deserve love, so you stick with whoever you got, and Michael was who he had.

Gage pulled his hands together, tucking them under his chin, heavy in thought about their last night together. *Damn, but they had gotten drunk that night.* A new gay bar, for leathers and bears, was having a grand opening party and they went. It was full up, wall to wall of furry mancandy. And dancing in the sea of them had them both lit up and hungry. They tore up the dance floor, and perhaps a bathroom stall, too, before they left. They at least played it smart and took a cab home, then fucked like rabbits.

Sometime before dawn, Michael decided to go out for cheeseburgers—

—he never came back.

Gage had always desired larger fuzzier men in his bed. Now pushing forty, Gage's arms ached all the more to hold a Teddy Bear he could keep.

He sighed heavily, patted the head stone then got to his feet, and headed back for the parking lot. The funeral up top was over. Two workers were taking down the green pop-up roof, loaded up in a golf cart, and left. Later, they would come back, afterhours, with the front loader and shovel the dirt in. Gage knew the drill.

The man and the priest, no longer in sight.

Gage loaded up on his bike and took off out of the parking lot. He hadn't made it a block when he spotted Boomer walking with a sullen stride down the sidewalk. He checked his mirrors, then changed lanes when it was clear, and pulled over beside him. "Hey, Boomer? You need a ride?"

Boomer stopped, looked at him, but his eyes flickered over his shoulder to the cemetery behind them. Gage's heart sank. That's why he kept looking to that lone man; it had been Boomer out there. "Boomer— you okay, man?"

Boomer just stood there; his hands pushed down into the front pockets of his jeans. The sleeves of his long john shirt poked out beyond the rolled sleeve of his flannel shirt. The white contrast against the nutmeg hair on his arm held Gage's eyes captive and it didn't even dawn on him that Boomer wasn't exactly in formal funeral clothes. Then again, maybe Boomer didn't own those kinds of things.

"Here, let me give you a ride home." Gage curled his fingers in, hoping to draw Boomer to hop on the bike with him. Still, Boomer just stood there, as if unsure of what to do with himself.

Gage had a sudden flashback of Boomer hanging up the picture of his mother at the gym; he missed a day and suddenly was hanging a picture of her up after all these years. *FUCK.* Gage cursed himself. *How stupid? Home* was probably the last place Boomer wanted to go. He was a loner, so the only person he'd be going to see buried was— *his mom.*

*Good God, Gage hoped he wasn't right, but just in case—* "Hey, I got a better idea. Why not come over to my place? We'll have a few beers and just hang." And like a lost child that had been given orders in a language he understood, Boomer stepped up and swung his leg over the back of the motorcycle behind Gage.

Gage steadied the weight, giving Boomer a moment to get situated, but the big man never moved again, his hands still stuffed in his pockets, sat frozen and blank. Gage lowered down in his seat, reached back taking one of Boomer's hands, pulled it free of the jeans and pulled Boomer's arm to wrap around his waist then did the same with the other side. Unsure of how to act or help, he just went on with what he offered, to take Boomer to his place. He footed the bike into first and pulled back out in traffic.

At first, Boomer hardly responded, his arms merely staying where Gage had put them, but as they passed by houses and cars from one tree lined street to another, Boomer's arms started to coil around tighter until Gage felt the bearded cheek drop over his shoulder and press into him. *I got you, big guy,* Gage thought to himself.

When he reached his street, he cruised right passed it and drove around half the day like that, just so they could both enjoy the mindless escape. He knew all the right neighborhoods to go through, too. Timeless subdivisions when boys used to play baseball in the street or at a nearby park just a few blocks down. Little girls played hopscotch in their mother's heels and men mowed their own lawns, adding the smell of fresh cut grass to the fragrant flowers of a manicured flower garden. And somewhere along their ride, Gage could have sworn he smelled fresh squeezed lemonade.

He rode them out towards the shores, were they sucked in the salty air of the ocean and seagulls flew over head with a cackle of calls. They made only a brief stop to gas up and grab a soda. Boomer never said a word, but as they took off again his arms went back around Gage's waist, this time without any prodding.

Gage rode them nowhere and took his time as he did so. Occasionally reaching down to stroke the furry arms still wrapped around him. Or to pat the thick leg that pressed against his own.

The afternoon sun splintered through the overhang of large, live oaks that guarded the sidewalks on both sides of the street. The city's Brownstones and rundown apartment buildings gave way to large New England style homes trimmed with green lawns. Purple Birch trees and Blue Cedar Pines added color and reminiscent memories as a kid trying to climb them. While neither of them lived in such comforts, it didn't prevent some calming nostalgia at the moment, and perhaps some wishful dreaming, too.

When he felt the grumbling hunger of Boomer's stomach against his back, Gage knew it was time to stop. They passed a few restaurants, but Boomer's lack of movement told him the big guy just wasn't up for being out in public like that. Gage thought perhaps he could stop somewhere and pick something up, but he feared Boomer might take off during the wait. So, Gage headed straight for home. If nothing else, he could order a pizza and hope it was the right thing rather than the worst thing to do.

Gage pulled up in the driveway of the small little box house that was his home. It wasn't much, but it was his.

Boomer got off and right away, his hands went into his pockets as he glanced around first at the house then down the street. Gage stood right away and risked taking hold of Boomer's arm to quiet any thoughts of running away. "Come inside, Boomer. It's actually pretty comfy in there. And I can get you a beer if you like." To Gage's relief Boomer followed him in and helped himself to one end of the sofa. He sat there for a moment, staring into space. His beer sweating with condensation, though he made no immediate move to open it or drink. Then suddenly his eyes flickered, and he leaned forward scooping up the DVD rental Gage had picked up on his way home the night before.

"The Incredibles," Boomer read aloud not looking at Gage or exhuming any form of emotion.

"After you told me what it was about, I went and picked it up."

"How come?"

Gage pursed his lips with a slight shrug. "I wanted to know what the joke was about so I could play along too."

Boomer fell quiet again and Gage let him. They sat in silence for some time, even after the pizza was delivered; Boomer just sat and stared at it. Gage didn't bother pushing it on him. He didn't gather the man really had an appetite for eating right now. No matter what the stomach said. But the silence was killing him. So, he risked the ultimate question. "Say, Boomer—?"

"My mom died this week," Boomer answered before Gage could get the whole thing out. "She came down with pneumonia. It was like the fifth time she'd had it in like two years. Only this time sh-shee—" the last of the words lodged up in his throat and never came out. If he let them, Gage was certain the man would start to sob. Not that Gage saw anything wrong with that. It was okay to cry about family.

"That's why you weren't at work Monday?" Gage asked just to keep him talking some.

Boomer nodded.

*Good enough.*

"Why didn't you tell any of us? At least Schiller?"

Boomer's head lobbed up and down in a slow rocking motion that was barely noticeable at first, "He called that night."

Well damn, maybe he could at least let Schiller know that he did care and would appreciate news like that; then again, maybe Schiller felt it was no one's business, especially when Gage had previously announced he was shipping out. But with his staying on, he hoped that would all change eventually.

All of these sudden thoughts rummaged through his head. *Wishing and hoping—* making plans. But he couldn't help himself. There was just something about the big, fuzzy giant that tugged on him and after the other night being in his grip, even if it was just for some shower play, Gage held foolish hopes for more.

Gage watched as Boomer finally popped the beer open and downed it in a near single swig and without asking, Gage got up to fetch a couple of fresh ones. He was just turning away from the fridge when he nearly plowed right into Boomer.

Gage wasn't exactly sure what to say or think so he just stood there looking at him. Hell, he wasn't even sure if it was kosher to reach out and hug the man.

"I just wanted you to know— the other night— I— uh, it was nice, and I mean, I'd been kinda wanting to for some time. I'm not what most guys want me to be, so I'm used to rejection. But, with mom sick, I didn't dare—" Boomer drew in a deep, heavy sigh letting it out just as slowly. He shifted on his feet, his eyes searching for something else to look at. His hand came up and fiddled with his thick beard and Gage couldn't help but think the timid shyness was rather cute on the big fella. Boomer was trying to figure out this talking shit and wasn't too comfortable with it. "I'm not like other guys," he repeated.

"I know, Boomer and it's okay, you don't have to be like everyone else. It's also okay to be gay."

Boomer swallowed as if that wasn't so easy a pill to swallow, "Being marched to the door by shotgun by your foster dad has a way of telling you otherwise. My mom was something special and I kept my life simple so she'd always fit in." Boomer let out another exasperated and exhausted sigh. "Anyways, I was— well, I mean, the other night— it wasn't just grief sex."

If Boomer was having issues with just finding something to say, Gage was having an even tougher time coming up with something to respond with— so far, everything he'd thought up in his head in that millisecond was downright cheesy. So, instead, he just grabbed Boomer's fuzzy cheeks and pulled him down to kiss him— gently.

And then he felt Boomer's beefy arms come around him and hang on, felt the large palms flatten on his back and press them tighter together. Hell, even if it had been grief sex, Gage would gladly have done it again. But that's not where this kiss took them. Moments later the kiss broke, and Gage found himself just holding Boomer. The man felt like he was going to collapse in his arms any minute, his body was just simply waiting for reality to catch up with him.

Gage pulled back and held up the two bottle necks still in one hand and waved them. Boomer nodded taking one and went back to the sofa, where they sat again in silence. Gage could tell it was only a matter of time and the bottom was going to come out from under Boomer's feet. At least he would be here with him when it happened.

Every now and then Boomer would shake his head, or a smile would break over his face as he recalled certain memories in silence. Gage could only watch. Wishing he could see inside the man's head but wasn't going to interrupt to ask. Sometime later, Boomer started to chuckle, the inward laugh then produced a tear that released all the emotions he was holding in.

And Gage decided to prod anyways, "What's so funny?"

Boomer brought his hand over his eyes and wiped the tears with thumb and forefinger, then paused to just shade them while a few more made their escape. "Something my mom used to always say."

"Yeah? And what was that?"

Boomer chuckled again, dropping his hand and looked at Gage. "People with freckles taste good."

"Like pumpkin pie?"

Boomer nodded, "Heavy on the nutmeg." His thumb scratched against his brown chest hair, while his eyes fell to the freckles that covered Gage's skin, then dropped his hand over Gage's. His finger idly tracing over a few of the speckled dots.

Gage chuckled softly. "Maybe that explains why she licked me."

"What?" Boomer looked up with a gaping expression then shook his head, "Dammit, I told her not to."

The air drifted quiet between them for a long pause, one that Gage wasn't sure was good. Boomer had said something about used to being rejected. Gage could feel there was so much more inside Boomer, only Gage wasn't sure how to open the bottle without scaring him off or making a blunder of himself as he tried to show that he cared. "Maybe she was trying to tell you something," Gage suggested, turning his hand over and taking Boomer's hand in his.

Boomer glanced away, his eyes darting about for something to zero in on. Gage watched or rather studied him, watching Boomer's chest heave with a deep inhale that was likely being converted into walls to block the pain and turmoil inside.

"What other kinds of things did she used to say?" Gage spoke, hoping to keep Boomer opening up.

Boomer pursed his lips then forced a grin, "Big hearts need big spoons." He nodded and the pain struck his face and that's when Boomer's walls broke. The sobs of mourning the little woman who loved him unconditionally with a childlike brightness, but who was now gone and left him abandoned to the world, rattled out of his chest and Boomer dropped his face into his hands. Gage reached over to catch him, pulling him over in his arms, and held him.

Boomer surrendered to him. Something one would never think to receive from a man his size.

When his sobs subsided, Boomer turned to look up at him and Gage found himself wanting to kiss him just then and so he did; nothing lustful or demanding, but slow, mushy kisses that found soft lips pressing back. The curls of Boomer's beard tickled delightfully with each one and when

Boomer's mouth opened to welcome him inside, Gage gladly accepted. Just hugging and kissing this giant felt good, until they were breathless. Then quietly, Boomer buried his face into Gage's shoulder, his body let out a heavy sigh and he surrendered to Gage's arms and the stroking caress he gave Boomer's back.

"I don't have any place to go." Gage heard him say in the safety of the hiding spot of his body.

*That was it,* Gage took over from there and he leaned Boomer back in the other direction of the sofa, pulling both their legs up alongside of his, and then rolled Boomer over to his side to spoon up against him. "Stay with me and let me be your Big Spoon for now." Gage whispered, wrapping his thick arms around the even thicker man. But no matter, he had him in his arms and that was everything.

They lay there in silence. Feeling each other's breathing level out to match the other's and the heartbeat that thumped from Boomer's back against Gage's chest was a connection every man hoped for, even when he's not ready to admit it. But Gage was ready. All his life he had wanted something more, a big Teddy Bear of his own.

"Can I stay here— for a while?" Boomer asked in the comfort of the darkroom, breaking the silence between them.

At that very moment, Gage felt himself falling deeply in love with this man. Every heart string plus a few he never knew existed, were plucked and humming in tune with the breathing creature in his arms. He wasn't sure if he'd be able to let him go if Boomer tried to move away.

He glanced up at the shelves on the wall across from them to the single framed photo of Skye standing on the podium with her gold metal sitting in the center of it. Maybe his shelf could have a photo of a boyish bear with his mom, too.

He tightened the hug around Boomer, hoping to say as much and rubbed his face against the back of Boomer's head, enjoying every bit of the snuggle embrace he had being Big Spoon. It just felt right to be here, and he hoped *here* was going to last a long— long while. It felt like home, and he whispered back, "God, I hope you stay a lot longer than that, Teddy Bear."

*Maybe for a gay ginger covered in pumpkin spice freckles, love with the right fuzzy Bear wasn't a pipe dream after all.*

# THE END

# DON'T STOP YET

# YOU'RE GONNA LOVE THE BONUS STUFF!!!

# Recipe Bonus

## CITRUS GLAZED PUMPKIN SPICE BREAD-PUDDING

1 ¼ cups milk

½ cup sugar

½ teaspoon pumpkin-pie spice

½ teaspoon cinnamon

½ teaspoon nutmeg *(optional)*

3 large eggs, lightly beaten

1 -15 ounces can pumpkin

4 ½ cups (1/2 inch) cubed challah or other egg

    rich bread (about 8 ounces)

Cooking Spray

1 large fresh orange (or 2 smaller size) *(we use*

    *local organic oranges – it's so worth the extra*

    *few dollars)*

1 cup of powdered sugar

1 tablespoon of softened butter

Combine first 7 ingredients in a large bowl, stirring well with a whisk. Add bread, tossing gently to coat. Spoon mixture into an 8-inch square baking dish coated with cooking spray. Cover with foil; chill 30minutes or up to 4 hours.

In separate dish: Grind whole oranges against a fine grater, then squeeze orange(s) for juice. Mix, cover and chill until ready.

Preheat oven to 350°

Place dish in a 13 x 19 baking pan; add hot water to pan to a depth of 1 inch. Bake covered at 350⁰ for 25 minutes. Uncover and bake an additional 10 minutes or until a knife inserted in center comes out clean.

In clean bowl mix soft butter and powdered sugar, then slowly start adding orange mixture 1 tablespoon at a time until you have a smooth glaze and poor over Pumpkin Spice Bread-Pudding and serve.

*(If you're not an orange fan, substitute topping with maple syrup and a few toasted pecans)*

# Bonus Read

# IVAN vs. IVAN

Gay Fiction / Mature – Bear Romance / Industrial
Blue-collar Theme / Suspense / Adult Content

Out here in the North Sea, love usually passes a man by like a ship in the night. So, it's a nice surprise when the captain of the ship hired to transport Ivan's ocean platform rig into port for the winter might actually offer some unexpected non-business type amenities as well.

Ivan Voloshyn owns and operates the *Marianna Shoal*, a deep-sea oil rig. It's hard work and long days out in harsh weather. And he loves it that way. Because that's what he knows. Seabeds— rigs— oil— and bad weather. He's also about to find out the Norse Gods have a sense of humor. For whom should it be to come riding in on the *Sea Dock* Heavy Lift ship? Another Ivan.

Captain Ivan Blažević knows who he is and what he wants; problem is, he also knows he can't have it. Just because the rest of the world is coming out of the closet doesn't mean every gay man can or should. Out here on the seas, the weather can change in an instant. He needs to trust his crew to do their job, and their hostility towards gays would get in the way of that if he was ever found out.

*Ivan-the rig-owner's* very presence threatens Blažević's closet doors, nevertheless it's hard to turn that away, because he wants him to keep doing so.

Out here, the North Sea can change a man's life—but hatred can take it away.

## EXCERPT

*Damn-beetches, he was in a lot of trouble now.*

He made a brisk inhale and just stared at the paused image. Frozen in time were two large burly men in what was clearly a full-on indulgence of gay porn. One actor on his back with his feet held up in the air by the other, who was balls deep in his ass.

Ivan spotted the remote and once more wasn't thinking his actions through as he stepped in and grabbed it up. His thumb hardly hovered over the buttons before he punched play. The paused scene instantly turned animated, filling the room with the gruff sounds of the two actors going at it. He felt more blood charge south for his dick sending back a mayday for a hand assistance. The lucky two in the scene lost in their pleasure. *Must suck to enjoy one's job so much.*

He leaned back on the doorjamb and scrubbed the back of his hand across his mouth. Doing his best not to let it go where he really wanted it to. *This was no good, standing in the room of another man— wanting him. He should have grabbed some ass before coming out on this trip.* One of the porn actors even had a beard, making it really easy to imagine it was Ivan and him.

*Fuck me.*

His head screamed with all the trouble he was considering risking, wishing he could look away, except, for just a minute longer, he didn't want to. For just a minute, he liked not having to worry too much about it— and just enjoy.

The two in the scene were getting close. Their breaths turned deep and heavy as they panted and groaned. So caught up, Ivan almost didn't hear the boots coming up the metal catwalk outside. He quickly thumbed at the pause button seconds before tossing the remote on the bunk and rushed out of the quarters, pulling the drape just as the door to the office swung open.

Voloshyn glanced at him oddly when he saw his guest wasn't where he'd been left— and then the growling shout of a man cumming came from behind the curtain.

Ivan was sure he felt his face turn white. He gripped the doorjamb behind him. It was all he could do not to bolt. *But go where? High dive off the portside?* He was frozen up something hard— like a wrench had been tossed in his gears and jammed him up, just like the supposed top-drive Voloshyn had to go tend to. Or rather, hard like his dick was, listening to the two actors vocalize brute ecstasy from the video— while he was staring at the sexiest fucker, he'd laid eyes on in quite some time. Or the fact he hadn't gotten any ass in an even longer time.

*Ivan-the-rig-owner* stepped around him and pulled the curtain aside, glancing in his quarters to see his porn scene had now played out, the two actors busily licking up their post evidence. He looked at Ivan and, without a skip, griped, "Now I'm gonna have to rewind it to get back to my favorite part."

Ivan swallowed, keeping his gaze with a set of blue eyes that belonged to a Norse god. All he could think was —*so close, I could kiss you right now. Drive my tongue into your mouth and steal the coffee I smell from your breath,* and— he swallowed again because Voloshyn wasn't even leaning away. Like he saw Ivan's thoughts or wanted them to come up. Ivan was out-right busted and now being called out on it. "And *vw*hich part is that?"

Voloshyn smirked. "The part where he gets bent over the desk and asks to be pounded."

# TIME: WOUNDS ALL HEAL

MM-Gay Romance/ Mature Men's Romance /
Suspense / Political-War Theme

*The Skeptic: "If all this had truly been staged, people would've figured it out and demanded the government come out about it."*

*The Journalist: "It's easy to fool a person— It's quite another to convince them they've been fooled."*

Even with the blanket of tattoos that covered both his arms and most of his upper chest, or the face hidden under the hair that constantly fell over his eyes, Channing Maroussas was likely the most beautiful man Chris Sayer had ever met. He was thankful they were close friends as it excused him for any lingering glances. Channing was a bird of brightly lit feathers perched in a world of darkness. But his gift wasn't just about being beautiful; it was what he could see. He could be in a room full of people, a field emptied of life, reading a newspaper, or overhearing a conversation on the bus— and what was unseen and unheard by others spoke volumes to him. Channing saw what the rest of the world never slowed down long enough to notice, though once pointed out, furies and passions flourished. It was voices like Channing's that broke the silence of ignorance. His voice just happened to be recorded between the pages of TIME magazine.

Chris Sayer has known Channing for years. But not even that can broker some rules of silence. Chris's government job is so secretive he can't even tell his best friend who he works for, which doesn't help his disagreement over Channing's journalistic views on global current events. He likes it even less when he finds out Channing left for Syria to cover a story. After Channing accusing the leading presidential elective Nolan Prumpt of inciting hate mongering and fascism, a trip through the greatest hot zone on the planet was like wanting to wash a pill down with poison. But when news got out that Channing had gone missing, Chris knew better than to believe the accusations that his best friend may have changed sides and was now considered an enemy of the state. The one thing Chris did know was he needed to do everything in his power to find Channing before anyone else did. If for no other reason but to let him know how he feels about him.

Time— it's not long enough — yet with enough of it, wounds all heal.

# THE TEDDY BEAR COLLECTION

Their Plane from Nowhere

Big Spoon & Teddy Bear

Ivan vs. Ivan

TIME: Wounds All Heal

Shaggin' the Dead

# COMING SOON TO COMPLETE THE COLLECTION

Life w/ Missing Parts

Chris Kringles' Magic Christmas Socks

# About the Twins

We Came— We Saw— and then we took you on an adventure.

Both Proud Indy Authors: Tarian like his twin, Talon, love to torment their editor with a nefarious world of foreign-language, slang, local dialect, stretched/outside-of-the-box definitions, and have even been known to throw in some new word creations of their own at times. This, of course, is all thrown in there with the dyslexia soup stock they both suffer from that makes editing for them a joy {joy: n. see mental illness}.

However, the final product comes out as richly detailed as we believe all stories should be created: holographic worlds of love, pain, frustration, and challenges beyond the every day. We believe a good story should take you on an emotional ride, pluck your heart strings, and zing you about until you're dizzy and screaming at the antagonist, while cheering for the protagonist before returning you to your cozy reading spot. And we've created these adventures within a mix of genres, so you can find the one right for you: Gay & Het Romances, Suspense, Paranormal and Sci-fi Erotic Romances, War-time Romance Fictions, along with Talon's favorite Space Sci-Fi Frontiers, and Tarian's favorite works of Post-Apocalyptic Dark Fantasies and Historical Fantasies. All for readers to submerse themselves into and escape from their day when they need or desire, and to whet your appetite for more.

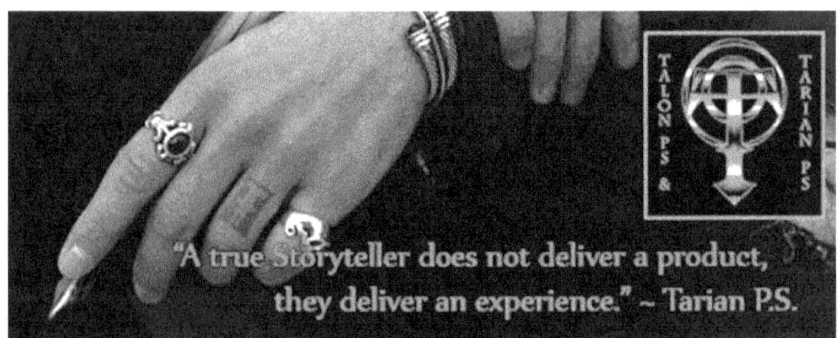

# DISCOVER THESE OTHER TITLES BY TALON PS & TARIAN PS

## DOMINION OF BROTHERS SERIES
Becoming His Slave
Domming the Heiress
A Place for Cliff
Rough Attraction
Taking Over Trofim
Right One 4 Diesel
Touching Vida~Vince

## LA SERIE DES FRERES DU DOMINION – (French Edition)
Devenir Son Esclave - Partie 1 & 2
Dominer l'Heritiere
Un Havre pour Cliff
Attirance Brutale

## QUANTUM MATES:
Pt 1~ What Torin Wants

## DEAR SOLDIER SERIES:
Dear Soldier, With Love
Dear Soldier, With Love II: A Lost Soldier Named Grey


## LYCOTHARIAN COLLECTION:

Bond of the Lycaon Concubine

TALON's KEEP COLLECTION:
Feral Dream by Talon PS
Danny's Dom by Nick Hasse

That's My Ethan

Muse Me Only
Inspire Moi Seulement (French Edition)

THE TEDDY BEAR COLLECTION:
Their Plane from Nowhere
Big Spoon & Teddy Bear
Ivan vs Ivan
TIME: Wounds All Heal
Shaggin' the Dead

THE SADOU ORDER – A Dark Taboo Short
Perfect Boy / Perfect Son

TARIAN ALSO WRITES UNDER THE FOLLOWING PEN
NAMES FOR SEPARATE GENRES:

as STEPHAN KNOX ~ HISTORICAL FANTASY AND POST APOCALYPTIC SCI FI

Anáil Dhragain (Dragon's Breath)

Keeping With Destiny

as ROCK HARDING ~ ADULT COLORING BOOKS

The Adventures of Hugh Jorgan

CONNECT AND FOLLOW THE TWINS:

WWW.TALON-PS.COM

THE TWIN'S FACEBOOK AUTHOR PAGE

TALON ON GOODREADS / TARIAN ON GOODREADS